"All right, Bradenton," the constable began. "Now's your chance. Stand up and face your accusers."

Accusers wouldn't have been the word Grace chose, but with what the constable faced day in and day out, it made sense. She shifted to stand alongside her uncle as the man in question rose and lifted his head. A soft gasp escaped her lips. She didn't expect this at all.

The offender couldn't be more than five or six years her senior. Not a lad at all, and not a hardened criminal. And she'd been right about his apparel. Judging from the way he held himself, just shy of her uncle's six-foot-two height, he came from some level of refinement.

But where was the smug expression? The cold, steely eyes? The haughtiness of a successful robbery executed with precision? Grace couldn't find a single shred of any of that in his contrite eyes. Instead she saw true remorse in their depths. Warm, with flecks of golden rays, like a fine glass of brandy.

And those penitent eyes held her captive.

D0874977

AMBER STOCKTON

is a freelance web designer and author whose articles and short stories have appeared in local, national, and international publications. Her writing career began as a columnist for her high school and college newspapers. She is a member of American Christian Fiction Writers and Historical Romance Writers. Some of her hobbies include traveling, music, photography, and MOPS. At age three, she learned to read and hasn't put down books since. She lives with her husband and fellow author, Stuart Vaughn Stockton, and their two children in colorful Colorado. Visit her website to learn more or to contact her: www.amberstockton.com.

Books by Amber Miller

HP784—*Promises, Promises*
HP803—*Quills & Promises*
HP823—*Deceptive Promises*

Books by Amber Stockton

HP843—*Copper and Candles*
HP867—*Hearts and Harvest*
HP883—*Patterns and Progress*
HP984—*Bound by Grace*

Stealing Hearts

Amber Stockton

Heartsong Presents

As always, I owe a great deal to my family for their continued support. A special thank you to my husband, who takes our little ones while I press toward the finish line of each deadline. To my editors, Jessie F. and Becky G., and the entire team at Barbour, this book would never have reached this point without you. To Joy, for your critique and polishing of this book.

A note from the Author:

I love to hear from my readers! You may correspond with me by writing:

**Amber Stockton
Author Relations
P.O. Box 9048
Buffalo, NY 14240-9048**

ISBN-13: 978-0-373-48630-4

STEALING HEARTS

Chapter 1

Brandywine, Delaware, 1890

"Richard! Come quick!"

At her aunt's shriek, Grace Baxton threw back the bed-clothes and tumbled to the floor of her bedchamber with a thud, the pain of impact sending a searing burn from her left elbow to her shoulder. The faint sounds of commotion downstairs penetrated her groggy mind and sent Grace into action. She made a frantic attempt to de-tangle herself from the mass of sheets and coverlets, only imprisoning herself further before escaping. At nineteen years of age, regaining her equilibrium turned out to be harder than she'd thought. Finally free, she jumped to her feet, grabbed her wrapper, and raced from the room, fastening the belt as she ran toward the main staircase.

She held tight to the banister, lest she stumble again, and caught sight of her uncle rushing from the direction of the drawing room, the sides of his unfastened black wool smoking jacket flapping back against his arms. Grace followed close on his heels the moment her feet touched the lower floor of their home.

"Charlotte, what happened?" Uncle Richard spoke without preamble the moment he entered the formal dining room.

"See for yourself." Aunt Charlotte extended her right arm toward the three-door vitrine cabinet with the mirrored backing. "Elise alerted me only moments ago."

Grace stood and stared, her tightened throat making it almost impossible to breathe. The blood drained from her face, and she grabbed hold of the nearest Queen Anne chair to alleviate her sudden light-headedness. Raising her other hand to her face, she wiped the sleep from her eyes, blinked several times, and fought back a yawn. Grace couldn't wrap her mind around the truth. The maidservant must be mistaken. One of their male servants always remained downstairs at night to prevent such an occurrence. Yet no manner of denial would erase the reality her eyes beheld at that moment.

How could something like this have happened? And while they all slept comfortably in their beds, completely ignorant of the intruder one floor below, making his way through several rooms and probing through their personal possessions. It made Grace's skin crawl, and a shiver traveled up her back.

Robbed.

Even just thinking the word brought a sour taste to Grace's mouth. She wet her lips and swallowed several times—as if that would make the circumstances less grave. Not exactly a desirable way to begin this cool May morning.

"Aunt Charlotte?" Grace croaked. "Your filigree China?"

"And my fine silver." A pause. "The tea set as well."

Her beloved aunt clutched an embroidered handkerchief to her lips. Her russet locks fell in soft waves down her back, evidence of a morning hair-pinning interrupted. She moved her hand away from her mouth and turned pain-filled eyes toward Grace.

"But that's not all," Charlotte added.

Grace followed her aunt's gaze toward the curio cabinet in the corner. Her right hand flew to her mouth as a gasp escaped.

"No!" She stared at the empty case, the tightening in her chest returning. "Not the books, too." Her aunt had spent a great deal of time tracking down several of those titles. And one in particular had been in the family for generations. Surely they weren't as valuable to the thief as the silver and dishes. "Why would someone steal those?" Whoever robbed them couldn't have known of their sentimental value. "They are precious to us, but to some unknown vagabond?"

"I can scarcely believe it myself." Charlotte waved her fingers and beckoned Grace to come closer. The woman who had been like a mother to her for the past eight years wrapped an arm around Grace's shoulders.

Her aunt wasn't one for verbose speech, but her unspoken actions said more than any words could. Grace draped her left arm around her aunt's waist and leaned her head onto the woman's shoulder, offering what comfort she could. Charlotte tilted her own head to rest her cheek against Grace's hair. The action made Grace self-conscious of her own state of undress and unkempt appearance. She reached up to touch her tousled caramel ringlets, grimacing at the telltale knots in desperate need of a brush. Harriet would see to that soon enough. They had more important matters at hand.

"What are we going to do?" Grace spoke to no one in particular.

Uncle Richard came to stand on Aunt Charlotte's other side and placed a hand on her shoulder, giving his wife a gentle squeeze.

"First things first, we are going to send Matthew for the constable." His voice took on a decided edge. "Then I will send out Bartholomew and Marcus to pay a visit to the area pawn broker shops. Whoever this thief is, I cannot imagine he would have taken all of this for himself." Uncle Richard fastened his jacket. "If we act quickly, we may very well have a chance to retrieve some of these items."

"Oh, Uncle Richard, do you truly believe that's possible?" For the first time that morning, a glimmer of hope entered Grace's heart. Perhaps those precious books weren't lost forever.

"Only time will tell, Grace, but we will not leave a single stone unturned in our quest to return our possessions to their rightful place."

Aunt Charlotte pulled away from Grace and moved to stand facing her husband. Uncle Richard immediately pulled her to him and placed a lingering kiss on her forehead. "We will get through this. I promise."

"I know. It is rather disconcerting to be facing this, that's all." Her aunt closed her eyes and leaned against Uncle Richard. "Thank you for being my strength."

"Always," he replied.

Grace felt like an intruder on the private exchange. She took a step backward, intending to slip out of the room and leave them alone. A moment later, though, her aunt and uncle turned toward her and opened their arms at the same time in her direction. Grace stepped into their embrace and cherished the immediate security it offered—despite the recent breach of the place she'd always considered a safe haven.

"All right." Uncle Richard, the first to break his hold, cleared his throat. "Let me summon Matthew. Then we can finish seeing to our own preparations for the day." He offered them both a wry grin. "I daresay we would not want the constable to pay us a visit and find us in our present state of undress."

Aunt Charlotte's cheeks colored a rosy shade of pink, and she bit her lower lip as if just remembering her morning routine had been so rudely interrupted. "You are absolutely right, my dear." She turned toward her niece. "Come, Grace. We shall return upstairs, where Harriet and Marie will assist us. Then we can look in on Claire and Phillip."

Oh right. Her cousins. She had forgotten about them in all the commotion and unrest. Good thing they slept better than she did. Grace envied that in a way. There would be questions enough once the seven- and five-year-old discovered what had happened. For now, let them benefit from the blissful peace of sleep.

"Very good, Mr. Baxton." The constable flipped his notepad closed and tucked it inside his dark chestnut trench coat. "I believe we have everything we need to further pursue this investigation."

Grace peered around the corner from the doorway of the sitting room, her hands clenched around the smooth wood frame. Her uncle and the constable stood near the front door, wrapping up their conversation. Any moment now, her aunt would chastise her for eavesdropping and bid her to return to her seat. But she wanted to know what would be happening next.

"We appreciate your prompt arrival, Constable." Uncle Richard reached out to shake the officer's hand. "You can very well imagine our great distress first thing this morning when we discovered this had happened."

"Yes." His voice was grim. The man adjusted his wire-rimmed spectacles and slid his hand down to his trim handlebar mustache. He stroked the well-groomed hairs with his thumb and forefinger. "This is the fourth report we've had in the past fortnight. I do not wish to speculate, but it seems clear we have a serious situation at hand."

Uncle Richard's eyebrows rose. "Do you mean we are not the only ones to have suffered from such an unwelcome intrusion?"

"No." The constable let out a frustrated sigh. "And each report is the same. The items stolen are quite valuable, but they are always from just one room in the home. Nothing else is disturbed, and there are no traces left following the burglary. Not even the slightest hint of forced entry or evidence of whether more than one individual might be involved." He scratched his chin then dropped his arm to his side and hunched his shoulders. "It is aggravating, to say the least."

Her uncle slipped his hands into the front pockets of his wool frock coat. "I have to admit I was greatly surprised, but it is even more disconcerting to know this thief has struck other residences as well."

Grace shifted her weight from her left to her right foot and back again. She wanted to rush forward and ask about the other homes that had been robbed. But it wouldn't be proper to interrupt. Chances were, they knew at least one, if not more, of the families who had become victims. Why hadn't something like this made the rounds in drawing-room conversations during the past two weeks?

"Why are we hiding from Papa?" Claire's hushed voice sounded from behind Grace's skirts.

Grace glanced down to see her seven-year-old cousin peering into the main foyer, mimicking her own stance. "We aren't hiding, Claire. We're listening."

"What is Papa saying to the policeman? And if you want to hear, why don't you go into the hall and stand there with them?"

Uncle Richard paused in his response to the constable and glanced in their direction. Grace shrank back from the doorway, gently moving Claire back with her. "You need to be quieter, Claire. We don't want to interrupt your papa's conversation."

"Grace." Her aunt's tone inserted more into that one word than an entire scolding could achieve.

"Yes, Aunt Charlotte?" She turned and assumed an air of innocence. "Do you need something?"

"Do not attempt to sugarcoat your present behavior, young lady." Her aunt pursed her lips and dipped her chin while raising one eyebrow. "You know very well how inappropriate it is to listen in on a conversation of which you are not a part. You are acting more like a schoolgirl than a lady of nineteen. And you are being a rather poor example to Claire."

Grace glanced again at her cousin, who crossed her arms and delivered an adorable smug expression. She pressed her lips into a thin line to avoid laughing at Claire's antics and returned her attention to her aunt.

"You are right, Aunt Charlotte. Forgive me." Grace placed both hands on her thighs. Her palms pressed into the smooth silk of her light coral morning gown as she bent to be eye-level with her niece. "Claire, I was wrong to eavesdrop. We should be minding our manners. I apologize for leading you astray."

Charlotte wagged her forefinger in a beckoning motion. "All right, both of you come back here right now and take your seats." Aunt Charlotte aimed a glance at her daughter. "Claire, you have your morning studies to finish. And Grace, I would like you to assist Phillip with his letters." She returned to the correspondence on the small table in front of her. "We shall know soon enough what is transpiring in the foyer. I assure you."

Grace moved to stand behind Phillip at the longer table where the children did their schooling. In the autumn Claire would begin studies at the academy in Wilmington. And in just a few more weeks, the children would shift into their lighter schedule for the summer. That meant Grace could return to her uncle's shipping office several days a week to assist with the record keeping. Usually she worked with Aunt Charlotte at Cobblestone Books, or helped Aunt Bethany with the antique collections at Treasured Keepsakes. But the shipping office at the port in Wilmington? So many people, so many ships, all coming and going. Grace could hardly wait.

As Phillip painstakingly copied the words and letters from his lead sheet, Grace alternated between watching the doorway to the sitting room and her aunt. It appeared the anxious anticipation had also bitten Aunt Charlotte. Although seemingly engrossed in the current message she wrote, her aunt also cast surreptitious glances from the corner of her eye toward the foyer. Grace quietly cleared her throat, and her aunt looked up. This time Grace raised a single eyebrow, and her aunt gave her a sheepish grin. It felt good to know she wasn't the only one with an insatiable curiosity regarding her uncle's conversation. Her aunt merely concealed it better.

Sudden commotion sounded in the entryway. The front door crashed open and banged against the stopper on the floor. Raised voices tumbled over each other in a muddled clamor of frantic tones. All four of them jerked their heads toward the din. What in the world had caused such a ruckus?

Grace looked to her aunt, who had scooted to the edge of her seat, her white-knuckled hands gripping the sides of the wingback chair. Every fiber in Grace's body wanted to rush from the room to see the source of the disturbance. And just as she took a step in that direction, Uncle Richard appeared. His eyes immediately sought out his wife.

"They've found him." Excitement fairly radiated from his face. "The thief."

So soon? Grace straightened and looked from her uncle to her aunt. They'd just discovered the stolen items a few hours ago.

"But how?" Aunt Charlotte shook her head, closed her eyes for a brief moment, then opened them again, as if wrapping her mind around the announcement. "When? Where?"

"Marcus and Bartholomew just got back with the news." He jerked a thumb in the opposite direction. "Seems the thief didn't cover his tracks very well. A few of the items were recovered at the third shop our young men visited. Since word spreads quickly among those brokers, when the guy attempted to sell a few more items at a different shop, the owner detained him and contact the authorities."

That was it? All the restlessness and turmoil of the morning ended just like that? Grace should be relieved, but somehow it all felt so anticlimactic.

Aunt Charlotte's shoulders dropped, and all tension

disappeared from her body. "So, we will soon have our items returned?"

"Not all of them." Uncle Richard stepped farther into the room. "We have the tea set and the silver for certain. The rest, they haven't determined yet." He turned and gestured toward the foyer. "They are waiting for us to come to the shop and confirm our belongings…and to press charges."

So the crook was still there? And her aunt and uncle would come face-to-face with him? Grace wished it could be her. She knew vengeance was best left up to God, but God hadn't been wronged here. Her family had.

"Right now?" her aunt replied. "Do they need both of us present? Claire and Phillip are in the middle of their lessons."

"So, leave them in Sarah's capable care." He paused. "Or Grace could accompany me." Uncle Richard looked her way. "Since the items stolen will become hers one day, in a way, she has a vested interest in seeing them returned as well."

"Oh Richard, Grace does not need to be present at something like this."

"But, Aunt Charlotte, I want to go," Grace rushed to interject.

"Can I go, too?" Claire chimed in.

"And me?" Phillip added.

Uncle Richard chuckled and walked to the table where his children sat. He reached out and tousled Phillip's auburn hair then tapped Claire's pert nose. "Not this time, children. You heard your mother. You need to complete your lessons." He shrugged. "Besides, a dark and musty old pawnshop is no place for either one of you. And what we'll be doing wouldn't be of much interest. You would be much happier here at home."

"So, may I go?" Grace brought the conversation back to the unanswered question. "As Uncle Richard said, some of those items partly belong to me. And he might not be able to accurately identify everything anyway." She glanced at her uncle. "No offense intended, Uncle Richard."

He splayed out his hands. "None taken." Looking to his wife, he nodded. "Grace does have a point. It will be good to have one of you present to make certain everything is there."

Aunt Charlotte looked back and forth between her husband and Grace, appearing to weigh the pros and cons in silence. "Very well." She released a resigned sigh then pointed a warning finger at Grace. "But mind yourself and be careful. We *are* dealing with a thief, after all."

"I will." Grace maneuvered around the table to where her aunt sat and leaned down to place a kiss on her cheek. "Thank you."

"Excellent." Uncle Richard clapped his hands together. "Let us not waste any more time. I am sure the constable wishes to close this case and move on to other matters."

Grace wanted to get moving as well. The sooner they arrived, the sooner she could give this scoundrel a piece of her mind.

Chapter 2

Grace stepped into the shop as her uncle held the door for her. The musty smell assailed her nose at the same time the well-lit interior challenged her preconceived notions of pawnshops. Shouldn't they be dim and crowded, with acquired items in haphazard disarray on every available surface? This one bore evidence of a thorough and meticulous owner, not the smarmy sort Grace expected. At that moment, a portly fellow with a receding hairline appeared from behind a hung burlap curtain across a doorframe.

"Good day to you, sir, miss." He wiped his hands on a once-white apron and approached, extending his right hand in greeting. "The name's Bancroft. Jeremiah Bancroft. What can I do for you?"

The man seemed pleasant enough. But why would a man like him be running a shop like this? Why not something a bit more reputable?

"Good day, Mr. Bancroft." Uncle Richard shook his hand. "I am Richard Baxton, and this is my niece, Grace. We are here regarding—"

"—the stolen property from your home last night," Mr. Bancroft finished for him. "Yes. The constable alerted me to your coming arrival." He stepped toward a closed door. "We have the young man over here. Follow me."

Young man? Grace hesitated. Could the thief be a lad instead of a full-grown man? She didn't know if she could face someone younger than her and still maintain the same level of ire.

"Grace?" Her uncle touched her elbow. "Is everything all right?"

"Yes. I'm fine." Or at least she would be once they entered the next room. Then she could lay all her uncertainties to rest.

"Shall we?"

How could her uncle be so calm about all this? Grace scrutinized his face. From the well-groomed dark brows to the almost emotionless eyes, down the narrow yet prominent nose to the straight-line lips. And there it was. The miniscule tick in his left cheek. So, this imminent meeting affected her uncle more than he let on. And with good reason. Their intruder waited just beyond that door.

"Yes," she said with a self-satisfied smile. "We shall."

Bancroft nodded at seeing their readiness and placed his hand on the doorknob. With a quick turn, he pushed open the door and disappeared inside. Grace preceded her uncle by just a step or two. By the simple furnishings and decor, this must be the owner's office. On the plain oak desk sat her aunt's tea service and the silver, as well as a selection of fine china dishes. Her eyes immediately caught sight of the constable who had been at their home earlier that morning. He silently acknowledged them both and gestured toward the man sitting hunched in a chair against the wall, his head in his hands.

Now they would come face-to-face with the man who had broken into their home and threatened their sense of peace. Ironically he didn't look all that threatening or menacing. And the quality of his clothing didn't line up with the ragamuffin lot she'd heard combed the streets, seeking out opportunities to make a quick strike. In fact, if she didn't know better, she'd almost mistake this law-breaker for someone who walked the sidewalks outside their home on a daily basis. He lacked the vest, coat, and top hat, and perhaps a walking stick, but his tailored ivory shirt with thin stripes, walnut canvas vest, and sable cotton trousers balanced with that image. How did a man like this end up stealing from a family like theirs?

"Mr. Baxton, are these articles the ones in question?" The constable splayed his open hand toward the items collected on the desk.

Uncle Richard took two steps forward, and Grace took three. All of that definitely belonged to her aunt.

"Yes," her uncle replied. "These are them." His voice lacked obvious emotion, but Grace could hear the anger lacing his words. He glanced to his right at the man who still sat with his head hung low.

"I only see one complete place setting here of the china." Grace reached out to trace the salmon-shaded filigree pattern on the edge of one plate. "Is this all that could be recovered?" She looked up at the constable.

"That is all I had in my store," Bancroft chimed in from behind her. "Yes. But it is not uncommon for individual place settings to be sold this way instead of as a full set. Makes it easier to offload the wares and not raise as much suspicion."

"And now that we have the pattern," the constable

added, "we can search more specifically for the rest of the pieces." He captured her uncle's attention with his direct gaze. "Are we ready then? We need to move forward with the official charges."

Uncle Richard only nodded, but he inhaled a deep breath and clasped his hands behind his back as he turned toward the guilty party who was awaiting his sentencing.

"All right, Bradenton," the constable began. "Now's your chance. Stand up and face your accusers."

Accusers wouldn't have been the word Grace chose, but with what the constable faced day in and day out, it made sense. She shifted to stand alongside her uncle as the man in question rose and lifted his head. A soft gasp escaped her lips. She didn't expect this at all.

The offender couldn't be more than five or six years her senior. Not a lad at all, and not a hardened criminal. And she'd been right about his apparel. Judging from the way he held himself, just shy of her uncle's six-foot-two height, he came from some level of refinement.

But where was the smug expression? The cold, steely eyes? The haughtiness of a successful robbery executed with precision? Grace couldn't find a single shred of any of that in his contrite eyes. Instead she saw true remorse in their depths. Warm, with flecks of golden rays, like a fine glass of brandy.

And those penitent eyes held her captive.

Andrew should look away, should also acknowledge the older gentleman who stood beside the young lady. But something about the striking, crystal-blue eyes with a hint of gray left him motionless. With great effort, he broke the invisible connection and raised his attention to the man the constable had addressed as Mr. Baxton.

Now here stood a man with a silent command of authority. He kept most of his emotions from showing on his face. But the nonverbal cues said it all. The hands firmly clasped behind his back, the shoulders squared, and the angled chin raised just a hair communicated the man's disapproval. If Andrew didn't miss his guess, and if he could see behind the man's back, he'd also likely find Mr. Baxton tapping an index finger against his other hand with distinct precision. It reminded him of his own father, and the scene would probably play out in much the same manner once his father received word of Andrew's crime.

"Well, boy?" Constable Garrett spoke up, breaking the nonverbal standoff. "What have you got to say for yourself? Now that you can look into the faces of the fine people you robbed."

And there it was. The reminder of the criminal he'd become as a result of this hotheaded, solitary act. It had seemed like such a good idea at the time. The man who alerted him to the opportunity said it would be a sure thing. Breaking in had been quite easy. Almost too easy, now that he thought about it. If only he'd been smarter about disposing of the items he'd stolen. Maybe then he could have pocketed the money and not looked back. Andrew sighed. No sense pining for what he couldn't have. He'd been caught red-handed. And he had to confess.

Andrew squared his own shoulders. "Mr. Baxton, sir," he began, looking the man directly in the eyes. "I know you must be thinking a few things about me right now, and none of them are favorable." No, in fact, the man's thoughts probably obliterated any chance at him maintaining even a shred of good character. "But now that I stand before you, I have nothing left to say except, I am truly sorry."

Mr. Baxton didn't flinch, didn't move, didn't even

blink. He remained a solid statue, carefully watching. Andrew almost cowered under the man's silent degradation. Come on, he could do better than such a lame apology. Couldn't he?

"You have every reason to consider me among the most undesirable lot. To mete out the most detrimental of punishments for what I've done." Though Andrew prayed that wouldn't be the case. "All I can ask is for your forgiveness. What I did was reprehensible, but I hope not unforgiveable." All right, time to drive the point home. "Contrary to the evidence, this is not a regular habit of mine. In fact, it is the first time in my life I have ever done such a thing."

The man and the young lady with him both reacted to that. Baxton immediately looked to the constable.

"Is that true, Garrett? This young man isn't the one who also robbed the other homes in our area?"

"As much as I would like to deny it, I can't," the constable replied. "What Mr. Bradenton says is the truth. We found no evidence he'd ever done this before, and none of the shop owners had seen him at any time prior to this."

Baxton turned back to face him. "Then why this time? Why us?"

Should he answer that honestly? Why not? He had nothing else to lose. He'd already sullied his good name and would have to stand before a judge for sentencing. At least he could be candid with everyone. It might even help his case.

"To tell you the truth, sir, I made a rash decision because of my mother." Another startled expression from the young lady. And perhaps a bit of sympathy? "She's been sick for a while now, and she's had several surgeries. The doctors aren't sure what the problem is, but while they try to figure it out, their bills continue to come. My father never spoke of it, but I could see the strain taking its toll. He's too proud to admit we can't afford it all at once like this." Andrew splayed out his fingers and shrugged. "I was only trying to help." He sighed. "But now, I've just made things worse."

"I won't disagree with you there," Baxton stated in a no-nonsense tone. "The question is, what are we going to do about it?"

"That's a question *I* can answer," Constable Garrett said. "But first, Mr. Baxton, are you going ahead with pressing formal charges?"

Baxton hesitated a fraction of a second, and in that fraction, Andrew's hope rose. But the man's next words dashed that hope.

"I do not have a choice," he answered, his tone both stern and forgiving.

Andrew noted the obvious lack of the word *we*. He looked again at the young lady who had accompanied Baxton. Since introductions hadn't been formally made, he had no idea of her relation or connection to the older man beside her. Her bare left hand bore no evidence of a wedding band, and she shared a family resemblance to Baxton, although not an overt one. He also couldn't forget the way she'd held his gaze at the onset of their meeting. That alone ruled out a wife. So who was she?

The constable stuck his thumb almost into Andrew's chest and interrupted his musings. "Well, then Bradenton here has an appointment with the judge across the street. Now that we've confirmed the stolen items, we leave it up to the judge to decide." With precise movements, Garrett grabbed hold of Andrew's upper arm and propelled him toward the door. "Let's go."

Andrew didn't know what he expected of his "trial," but the informal gathering of no one but the judge and the five of them from the broker's shop didn't even come close. In no time at all, both sides had presented their cases, and the judge had made a few notes.

The judge reached up to remove his spectacles and rubbed the bridge of his nose. "Does anyone else have anything to say before I pronounce the sentence?"

Silence answered his question.

"Very well." The judge made a final note on the paper in front of him then leveled a direct gaze at Andrew. "Mr. Bradenton, it is both my recommendation and my direct order that you serve three months in the employ of the Baxton family as restitution for your crimes."

A sharp gasp came from the young lady, now hidden from Andrew's view. Work for the family he'd robbed? Face them day in and day out with the constant reminder of how he'd wronged them? He would have gasped, too, if he hadn't been determined to maintain a stoic attitude in the judge's presence.

"The extent and duration of the work to be completed," the judge continued, "will be left to the discretion of Mr. Baxton. But you shall remain in their employ for three months, and not a day less. Only then will your sentence be complete. Do I make myself clear?"

Andrew nodded. "Yes, sir."

"Very well." The judge raised his gavel. "You are all dismissed." He brought the instrument down with a single echoing thud against the surface in front of him. "Constable? Mr. Baxton? You both can see my assistant out front for the necessary forms you'll need to sign. Thank you all for coming in."

And with that, the trial concluded. Garrett again took hold of Andrew's arm to escort him from the courtroom. As they pivoted, Andrew caught sight of the young lady. He almost stepped back and stumbled from the onslaught of her silent ire. The compelling crystal-blue had been replaced with cold-as-ice depths. What had happened to make her so angry? Back at the shop, when he'd confessed and asked for forgiveness, he could've sworn there'd been sympathy in her eyes. But not now. He hadn't said anything different in front of the judge than he had at the shop.

Perfect. Not only did he have to be reminded daily of his crime, but he had to deal with the animosity of the young lady he still had yet to meet. At least it eliminated the possibility of any distractions while he served his time. He'd complete his sentence and that would be the end of it. Nothing more, nothing less. Andrew prayed the three months would pass quickly.

Chapter 3

Andrew paused by the nearly full barrel and set down the two pails of waste from the kitchen. Almost time for a new barrel. The wagon would be by later that evening to haul away the waste, but at the rate this one got filled, they might end up with three or four before the day ended. He ran the back of his hand across his brow and wiped the sweat on the rolled-up sleeves of his shirt. It shouldn't be this hot in the middle of May. The sun beat down on him in merciless fashion from the cloudless sky.

He'd been at the Baxtons' for only four days. So far he'd been up on a ladder to wash the outsides of all the windows on the upper levels of the home, scrubbed the floors in the scullery and the kitchen, and emptied the waste pails several times a day. He'd even cleaned out the mud and grime that had collected on the carriages following the recent spring rains. After a morning like this one, though, his mere four days felt like weeks.

With a deep breath, Andrew bent and grabbed the pails then hefted them over the split-rail fence and dumped out their contents. He turned his head and coughed at the stench from a half a day's waste all gathered in one place. Oh, the things he'd learned about the inner workings of a country house in the short time he'd been here. If he had to endure this particular task much longer, he didn't know how he'd last.

Of course, it was only by God's grace that Andrew had the luxury of serving his sentence under Baxton's watch. By all rights, he should have been sent off to the penitentiary in Philadelphia. From what he'd heard, the months of solitary confinement drove some men mad. Day in and day out with no human contact whatsoever, and meals shoved through a hole in the door of the cell? Andrew shuddered at the thought. At least here he had the house staff going about their daily business. Though he rarely, if ever, spoke to one of them, their mere presence comforted him and made him grateful for the judge's favor.

As he headed back to the house, swinging empty pails by his sides, Andrew recalled the final day leading up to his arrival. His father had been incensed, as expected. But concern for his wife tempered the elder Mr. Bradenton's ire.

"How could you do something so completely reckless and foolhardy?"

The man paced back and forth in his study as Andrew stood, head bowed and hands tucked into the pockets of his trousers. Even at twenty-four, he could be reduced to a mere schoolboy by one well-placed look from his father. Father had removed his coat but not his vest, and rolled up his shirtsleeves. That didn't make him any less intimidating, though, as he continued his rant.

"You didn't stop for one moment to think of anyone

else and how this rash decision would affect us. And the consequences!"

Another turn. Several long strides across the Aubusson rug. Then back to the original direction. Father halted halfway in his trek across the room and spun to face Andrew.

"You obviously see the error of your actions now that you've been caught." He gestured and Andrew would have received his father's backhand had he been standing in front of him. "But why couldn't you have thought about that *before* you went through with this impetuous scheme? Before such a black mark was made against our family? And before you broke your mother's heart when she heard the news?"

Andrew didn't have any words for his defense. Everything his father said rang true. He *had* thought only of himself. He *did* do the quickest thing that might result in immediate money. And worst of all, his actions *had* disappointed his mother.

"It is true," his father continued, his voice taking on a more forgiving tone, "the doctors' bills are accumulating. And I have been forced to withdraw funds from accounts that by all rights should be reserved strictly for you and your brother and sister."

His voice hardened again as he moved to his desk and placed both palms on the surface. He leaned forward to pin Andrew in his direct gaze.

"But that does not give *you* the right to go off half-cocked and cook up some lamebrained ploy, hoping to gain a fast sum. No." He straightened and tucked his thumbs into the pockets of his vest. "When you need money, you earn it. You don't steal to get it." His father's shoulders slumped a little. "I thought I taught you better than that."

"You did, Father." Andrew took a step forward then froze at the steely resolve in his father's eyes. "And I'm sorry…for everything."

Father waved off Andrew's apology and turned his back. "I do not wish to hear another word. At the moment, your confession and act of contrition is meaningless to me." He bowed his head. "I need some time to come to grips with all this. I believe it is divine providence that you will also be boarding with the Baxton servants during your sentence. It just might take me that long to set things right. And I shall have to find someone to replace you at the mill." His father dismissed him with a brushing of his hand at his side. "Now, go see your mother. We'll talk again before you leave."

That second conversation hadn't gone any better. If anything, Andrew considered that one worse on the guilt scale. He grabbed a shovel from the shed to dig and till an extension to the existing vegetable garden then headed to the plot, his mother's words replaying in his mind.

"You have brought a great deal of disgrace to our family, Andrew," she whispered. Her eyes closed, and she inhaled a ragged breath before slowly releasing it. The pain must be an almost constant companion these days. Mother reached out and patted his hand. "I know your heart was in the right place, but your head wasn't." She opened her eyes and regarded him with the severe yet tender expression only a mother could achieve. "The two must always be in alignment."

Andrew rotated his hand to clasp hers. "Mother, I know I have wronged you and Father. But worse, I have caused you greater anguish than even your physical pain. And I cannot apologize enough to make up for what I've done." He gave her hand a squeeze. "But I vow to make things right again. I promise."

Mother slowly nodded. "I know you will, son. Of that, I have complete faith." She tilted her head up just a bit. "Now, give me a kiss and be on your way. I will pray daily for you as you fulfill your obligations."

The image of his mother in bed, in pain, and dealing with the shame in the wake of his mistakes haunted him even now. But the knowledge of her daily prayers kept him going. He drew strength from them, comfort and peace. Father had also invited him to write, and Andrew would do that at week's end. At least he hadn't been cut off. Praise God for that.

A small shadow fell over the dirt Andrew tilled.

"Excuse me, Andrew?" One of the kitchen maids, Elsa, spoke up, though even at this close range, her voice could be termed meek at best. "I've been sent to tell you that when you're finished with this, Mr. Baxton wants you to clean out the stalls in the stables and polish the saddles in the side room."

Andrew's shoulders fell. Didn't he have stable hands for that? Just what were these servants doing in place of the chores he completed for them? They weren't sitting idle. But if the work he did only freed up the staff to do other tasks, maybe Baxton should hire more help.

"Thank you, Elsa. I will go straight there as soon as I'm done here."

Elsa bobbed a curtsy, either out of habit or because she knew the reason for his presence there. Servants usually did *his* bidding, instead of the other way around. What an ironic twist of fate had befallen him.

Once the maid had disappeared again into the house, Andrew put the finishing touches on the tilled ground, returned the shovel and other items to the shed, and headed across the back lawn. How long would Baxton come up with menial tasks like these before he followed through on his promise to move Andrew up to the next level?

"Now that you've met the principal house staff," Baxton had said, "and are aware of the members of my family, we'll start with the first of your assignments." Baxton led the way into the dining room and paused before the butler and steward. "Harrison and Charles will oversee the majority of your duties. Anything I'd like done will be relayed through them, or another servant. If you accomplish your tasks in a satisfactory manner, we shall discuss entrusting you with more." He pivoted to leave then paused and cast a glance over his shoulder. "As head of this household and overseer of a rather successful shipping business, trust me when I say there is an abundance of work to keep you busy for three years, let alone three months." Baxton raised one eyebrow. "Your hands will not grow idle."

That parting remark had lined up more in reference to his hands being what stole than with the day-to-day chores he now did with them. Grabbing hold of the two handles, Andrew swung open one of the doors and stepped inside the stables.

"So, the errant jailbird with deep pockets finally comes down from the high perch of the manor house to grace us with his presence." A jeering greeting came from within the surprisingly well-lit interior.

Andrew searched the stalls, nooks, and crannies for the owner of the voice. A few seconds later, a solid young man about his age stepped into view halfway down the center aisle. He wore a pullover work shirt and a pair of tan trousers with suspenders hooked up over his shoulders. The brown tweed cap over sandy-brown hair curling at his collar rounded out the image.

"Best if you know right now," the man continued, "I

call the shots in here." He came to stand less than two feet from Andrew and folded his arms. "The name's Jesse, and anything that's to be done goes through me first."

Jesse had obviously forgotten about the head coachman. Andrew held his grin in check. Even standing nearly toe-to-toe, he still had Jesse by about three inches. Not much cause for concern.

Andrew shrugged off the obvious baiting. "Well, I'm only here to muck out the stalls and polish the saddles. You won't have any trouble from me."

Not that Jesse could do anything anyway. Andrew didn't give him a chance to respond. He just headed for the wheelbarrow and pitchfork and set to work, grateful Jesse didn't follow.

Halfway through the stalls, though, a commotion behind him made Andrew turn. The wheelbarrow he'd filled a moment ago sat on its side, the contents spilled. Now he had to fill it again. At least the manure remained in a pile. Shouldn't take him too long. He didn't see anyone nearby, but Jesse's sinister cackle sounded from somewhere near the front. Guess the stable hand didn't intend to leave him alone after all.

With the minor setback behind him, Andrew finished the stalls and moved to the saddles. He had three of them done when Jesse popped into the room. The stable hand walked to the far corner and randomly picked up miscellaneous pieces of tack, inspected them, and returned them to their original spot.

What did he want now? Andrew tried to ignore him and return to his work, but the man didn't make it easy.

"Be sure you hang those saddles back on their hooks. We don't want no rodents sinking their teeth into the leather, and they sure don't need to be on the ground where they'll get wet and musty."

Andrew clenched his teeth, not looking up. "Not a problem. I assure you." After wiping clean the glycerin, he poured more oil onto the cotton cloth he held and rubbed it into the leather in circular motions. Sure was a good thing he'd spent some time with Charlie, one of their stable hands back home, or Jesse might have had more chances to mock him for not knowing his way around the stables.

"By the way," Jesse added, reaching out to lift one of the saddles away from the wall. "This one's going to need to be done again."

Andrew looked at the saddle Jesse held. It had a dirt streak right across the center of the seat. He'd done that one first. No way had he missed something so glaring. If Jesse didn't stop, he might find himself at the mean end of a pitchfork before long. Or Andrew might grab one of those bits and use it for something other than placing in the horse's mouth. He didn't move though. It would be better to wait Jesse out than make another rash decision like the one that had landed him here in the first place.

After several minutes, Jesse brushed past Andrew, nudging him on his way out. Andrew swallowed several times and squeezed the cloth in his hand while rubbing far more vigorously than necessary. He was here to pay his penance. But he wouldn't sit back and take vindictive behavior like that for long.

Chapter 4

"Where are you going?" Seven-year-old Claire broke the silence of morning reading time with her rather loud voice.

Grace turned from the doorway and looked at her cousin. "I am stepping out for some fresh air, and I believe I will go for a ride."

"Can I come?"

The little girl's book fell to the floor when she scooted to the edge of her seat. Her sweet pixie-like face and eager expression coupled with how she bounced in the chair could wear down even the most stalwart of souls. But Aunt Charlotte gave an almost imperceptible shake of her head.

"Not this time, Claire," Grace replied. "Perhaps next time." She raised her index finger and waggled it at her cousin. "*If* you finish your studies."

"Oh I will!" Claire scrambled from the chair to retrieve her book, hopped back against the cushions, and flipped open the pages to where she'd left off.

Grace chuckled and shook her head. Oh, to be so young and carefree. And to have desires appeased so easily.

"You can't finish and still go with Grace." Phillip spoke up from his secluded spot in the corner. "Grace is all done. You will take too long."

Even at five, he exhibited signs of greater interest in books or solo activities than outdoor exercise. Just like his mother. Claire, on the other hand, had as much of Uncle Richard as possible. And Grace couldn't fault that. She, too, loved being outside. Every chance she had, she took it.

"Well, I am almost done," Claire said, laying her book on her lap. "I could go if I wanted." She crossed her arms, jutted her chin in the air, and closed her eyes. "But I don't want to." A peek from one eye at her brother. "Not now, anyway."

Grace exchanged a silent look with her aunt. Those two were quite a pair.

"Have a nice time on your ride, dear," Aunt Charlotte said.

"I will."

A part of Grace wanted to wait for Claire to finish. Her cousin could be a lot of fun riding horses in the nearby park. She always pointed out so many things Grace overlooked, and seeing the world through the eyes of a young girl could be quite effective in reminding her to appreciate the simple things in life. But not today. After a morning receiving an endless line of callers inquiring about Aunt Bethany's upcoming sale on some of her restored furniture, Grace had had her fill of people. Today, she wanted solitude.

It didn't make sense why they came to Aunt Charlotte to ask their questions anyway. Shouldn't they be going to Aunt Bethany? Just because Charlotte put the announcement in both *The Morning News* and *The Evening Journal* didn't mean those inquiring should come to her. But come they did, and now Grace needed some time alone. So after having Harriet assist her with changing into her riding habit, Grace headed for the stables.

She paused just outside and breathed in the scent of fresh hay and horses. As she pulled open the door to step inside, the smell of leather, lye, and oil joined the bouquet of aromas assailing her nose. Some might not find the stables appealing. In fact, they might find the ever-present odor repulsive. To Grace though, it brought a great deal of comfort, and it remained her favorite place in the world.

"Will you be needing your horse saddled, Miss Baxton?"

Grace started at the unfamiliar voice and turned to her left to see the criminal sentenced to work for them coming out of the room where they kept the saddles. It had been a little over a week since the incident. She'd all but forgotten him. Today he wore clothing more befitting a stable hand or assistant to the groundskeeper. But even these clothes bore distinct markings of specific tailoring. What was his name again? Adam? Albert? Arthur? Andrew? Andrew. That was it. Andrew Bradenton. But where was Jesse? Or Willie? They usually had her horse ready and waiting.

"Yes," she finally answered. "Yes, I will. Thank you."

Andrew returned to the room and hefted a saddle from the hook like it weighed nothing at all. Grace tried not to stare, but with no other movement anywhere, her eyes naturally followed him. While he retrieved the bridle and blanket, she walked over to Pilgrim's stall. He already had his head over the wall awaiting her approach. A whinny and a snort signaled his pleasure.

Grace reached over the wall and scratched his forelock. "So, are you ready for another jaunt in the park, boy? A good stretch of the legs?" She leaned forward and pressed her head to his, rubbing her forehead against the coarse hair between his eyes. "Yes, I know you are."

Pilgrim dipped his head farther and nuzzled the front of her clothes, vigorously moving his head up and down. Grace laughed and grabbed hold of his jowls to look him straight in the eye.

"Silly boy." She gave his forelock a good rub. "You know I will scratch your head anytime. There is no need to use my shirtfront as a post."

Andrew appeared at that moment, and Grace caught herself before she jumped at his silent approach. Without a word he unlatched the door and stepped into the stall. In no time at all, he had Pilgrim saddled and the stirrups adjusted. Grace admired how he worked with smooth precision. He obviously knew his way around a horse.

"I'll lead him out for you," he said.

His eyes met hers for a brief moment. And in that moment, Grace again saw the remorse he'd shown at the pawn shop over a week prior. This man bore none of the telltale marks of a lawbreaker without a conscience. Instead, his expression and his actions spoke only of a silent apology. She followed a respectful distance behind as Andrew led Pilgrim through the door and into the shining sun. As soon as the two stopped, Grace came alongside her horse's left, reached for the reins, and prepared to mount. Andrew again appeared without a sound. He interlocked his fingers and stooped to give her a leg up.

Grace hesitated. Had it been Jesse or Willie, she

wouldn't have blinked an eye. She would have accepted their help without question. With a man who had wronged her family though, it changed things. When she didn't place her boot in his hands, he looked up at her. His eyebrow quirked, and the faintest hint of a smirk formed on his lips, as if he dared her in an unspoken challenge.

Just where did he get the audacity to grin at her that way? And how could he even think of attempting to taunt her in such a fashion? He should be acting the part of a subservient member of the household staff. Grace could accept behavior such as that from the staff she knew well, but Andrew? No. She refused to give in to his baiting and give him any sort of satisfaction.

Grabbing hold of her split skirt, she raised the hem just enough to place her boot in his hands. With surprising gentleness, Andrew helped her mount then adjusted the stirrups. As soon as he stepped back, she acknowledged him with a nod.

"Thank you."

She might not wish to engage in any form of lighthearted repartee with him, but she would never forget her manners.

"You are welcome, Miss Baxton." He glanced at the spattering of fluffy clouds in the clear blue sky before returning his gaze to her. "It's a good day for a ride. I hope you have a pleasant time."

Andrew held Grace's eyes for several moments before she broke the invisible connection and faced forward. Her heart pounded a bit faster than usual, and her breath came in shorter spurts. She had come here to take advantage of solitude. Just her and Pilgrim. Now she needed that retreat for more reasons than one.

Heading west from the manor house, Grace guided Pilgrim along the path paralleling the Brandywine River.

Her horse could walk this route blindfolded if she let him have the lead, and the knowledge of that fact brought a level of reassurance to her. It allowed her to venture out and free her mind of everything, welcoming the peace that washed over her.

The screech of a red-tailed hawk sounded overhead, and to her left, a crane flew just a foot or so above the water's surface, the swoop of its wings causing ripples below. That brought to mind Andrew and how easily he'd hauled the saddle from the hook and lifted it to Pilgrim's back. His feather-light touch against her boot when he'd adjusted her stirrups still left an impression, and despite her best efforts, Grace couldn't get him out of her mind.

He'd confessed his crime as not being a normal one for him. And he'd told the judge the same thing. His speech, his mannerisms, and the cut and quality of his clothing attested that he wasn't of the working class. So, why then had he lowered himself to the point of a common thief? Surely his family had other means of securing funds for their medical bills. Another relative, investments from the bank, or even money saved for the future. A man with a background obviously closer to Grace's than the riff-raff who frequent the local jails should have had multiple options available to him. So why steal? And why their house? How had he gained access anyway?

Grace mulled it in her mind over and over again as she rode. Since Pilgrim knew the trail so well, she allowed him free rein, enjoying the exhilaration of the wind in her face and the thrill of riding such a powerful steed. Far too soon, the time came to return to the stables. Aunt Charlotte would be calling her to the midday meal, and after that, she would head to the bookshop. Would Andrew also be there upon her arrival?

She didn't have to wait long to find out. From the sound of things, Jesse was somewhere inside.

"I warned you, jailbird, not to do anything without asking me first. There's an order to the way things are done here, and if you want to change it, you go through me."

Jesse's voice carried on the wind. The jeering name Jesse used gave away the recipient of the tongue lashing.

"And I know my orders come from Mr. Wyeth, the head coachman." That strong and confident voice belonged to Andrew. "He oversees everyone here in the stables. Mr. Baxton instructed me to report to him, and him alone. If you have any complaint regarding my actions, you will need to discuss it with him."

There it was again. The cultured quality to his speech. The sign that someone had taught him propriety in more ways than one. Grace walked Pilgrim into the fenced area and dismounted, giving her horse a pat on his neck. She didn't want to alert the men inside to her presence, so she tiptoed toward the open doors and continued to listen. Aunt Charlotte's reprimand for eavesdropping came to mind, but in this instance, Grace knew her aunt would likely do the same.

"Well, Mr. Wyeth isn't here right now," Jesse continued. "And that makes me next in command. You still haven't cleaned out the two stalls at the end, and there's the feed and water for the horses."

"And if I do all of that, what will that leave you to do?"

"So now you're trying to tell me what I'm supposed to be doing? You sure have some nerve. I'm tempted to report you to Mr. Baxton myself at the first chance I get."

The tone of Jesse's voice hardened, and a menacing edge laced his words. Grace had never heard Jesse talk like that. He'd always been nothing but kind to her, al-

beit a bit cocksure at times. But nevertheless, respectful.
Why all this animosity toward Andrew?

"Do what you will, Jesse," Andrew replied with a
non-chalant air. "It won't change the fact that I was not
told to water and feed the horses. So, I won't be doing it."

"Guess that means I'll have to teach you a lesson my
own way."

All right, enough was enough. Grace knew she needed
to intervene before Jesse did something he'd regret. She'd
seen Andrew, and she knew Jesse's size. Jesse didn't
stand a chance. She rushed inside, not even waiting for
her eyes to adjust from the bright sun.

"Jesse, you will do no such thing. And I will not have
you tormenting anyone working these grounds in this
manner."

"Miss Baxton!" Jesse immediately stepped back from
Andrew and turned to face her. "I didn't know you had
come down to the stables." He offered a forced smile.
"Have you come for your normal ride?"

Grace inhaled and released a slow breath. "No, Jesse.
I have just returned, and if you had been paying more
attention to your regular duties instead of deriding Mr.
Bradenton here, you would have realized that."

Jesse dipped his head and closed his eyes. She had pur-
posefully used Andrew's formal name to set him apart.
Jesse had noticed. Grace wanted to look at Andrew, to
see how he was taking her interruption, but she refrained.
He or Jesse might infer something that didn't exist, and
she needed to stay on task.

"I am of a mind to speak to my uncle directly regarding your behavior a few moments ago. But if you give
me your word it will not happen again, I will cease from
doing so…this time."

"Miss Baxton, you have my word," he replied through

clenched teeth. "And do forgive me. I know I was out of place."

Grace didn't bother to address the fact that him knowing his place and still acting the way he had were in direct opposition. He had apologized, and she'd leave it at that.

"Very well. Now, please return to your work, and leave Mr. Bradenton to his."

Jesse only nodded, but Grace didn't miss the narrowed eyes or the meaningful glare he gave Andrew on his way to the back of the stables. That wasn't the end of it, but at least she'd prevented it this time. After seeing Jesse disappear into one of the stalls at the far end, Grace turned to face Andrew.

"I am sorry you had to endure that. Jesse isn't usually like that, and I—"

"I would appreciate it if you would let me speak for myself," Andrew interrupted. "I am not an errant schoolboy who needs help fighting my battles." Anger fairly dripped from his words, and fire flashed in his eyes. "So please refrain from helping in the future."

With that, he pivoted on his heel and walked away. Grace stood, her mouth open, unable to come up with a response. She thought he'd appreciate her stepping in on his behalf. At the very least, it was her place. Jesse shouldn't be treating him like that, and she'd prevented an almost certain altercation. So why hadn't he been more grateful? She clenched her fists. He could have at least uttered a simple word of thanks.

Grace spun in the opposite direction. Next time she wouldn't rush to his aid. As he wished, she'd *let* him deal with his own fights.

Chapter 5

Andrew walked down the corridor from the direction of the dining room, where he'd just helped two footmen position a new buffet and service set then remove the old. He slowed his steps just before the foyer when he saw Miss Baxton enter through the front door. Harrison swung the door wider then held out his hand to take her wrap and hat as soon as she stood in the entryway.

"Thank you, Harrison." She graced him with a genuine smile and made eye contact with him.

"My pleasure, miss," Harrison replied with a nod and slight bow.

"Is my uncle in his study?" Miss Baxton removed her gloves and handed them to the butler.

"Yes, miss." Harrison stacked the gloves neatly with the hat and wrap. "He left your aunt in the parlor and went straight there about fifteen minutes ago."

"Very good." She smiled again. "I believe I shall speak

with Aunt Charlotte first then go see my uncle. He will no doubt appreciate the few moments of solitude. Thank you."

The butler only nodded this time, but then he winked, and Miss Baxton chuckled softly. They obviously shared a special rapport. Not many folks of the Baxtons' class would interact with their servants in such a manner. And from the way the servants responded to the family, the admiration and respect went both ways. Andrew thought of his own servants. They performed their duties without noticeable complaint, but how did they feel about his father or mother, or even him? He didn't know. And being here made him question his own treatment of those who served him.

Miss Baxton headed straight for him and halted when she saw him. Her expression clouded and a frown marred her dainty lips. Even her eyes took on a noticeable hesitation. Well, he couldn't stand there forever in a visual stalemate.

"Good afternoon, Miss Baxton," he said with a slight bow.

"Mr. Bradenton," she replied, her words clipped.

Silence again.

A moment later she flounced away and disappeared into the parlor, sliding the doors closed behind her. Now what had he done to deserve that kind of treatment? She'd been far more cordial the other day when she'd come to the stables for a morning ride. And she had almost responded to his unspoken teasing when he offered to help her mount.

Oh, the ride!

When she'd returned, she'd stuck her nose into that disagreement he was having with Jesse. Had all but upstaged him and made him out to be a milksop who couldn't fend for himself. And that's when he'd snapped at her. Sure, it had been a rash response, but she had it coming. She shouldn't interfere in a man's affairs without his permission. Still, no wonder she'd greeted him in such a cool manner. He'd do the same thing in her shoes…although he hoped never to be there. The mere thought of changing clothes so often, entertaining callers, and planning menus made his lips curl in disgust. Give him the mill and manual labor any day.

On the thought of manual labor, he had another job to do. He'd best get to it.

"Why did you pull the doors to, Grace?" Aunt Charlotte spoke from the settee where she sat with a teacup in hand.

Grace glanced back over her shoulder, as if she could see through the panels. If she could, would Andrew still be standing there? Or would he have left as soon as she did? What did it matter? She shouldn't give him a second thought, anyway. He was paying off a debt to her family.

"Grace?"

She turned to face her aunt. "Forgive me, Aunt Charlotte. I am afraid my mind wandered a bit."

"That much is obvious," her aunt said with a grin. "Now why don't you have a seat? Join me for tea, and you can tell me all about it." She extended her arm toward the empty seat opposite her and the tray of assorted sweet breads on the table.

"Thank you. I believe I will."

Once Grace sat and poured herself a cup of tea, her aunt leaned back against the settee. "Did you have a productive morning working with Aunt Bethany?"

Grace took a bite of a fruited scone and swallowed. "Yes. We managed to separate out the items she is going to be selling at the auction, categorize the items she has yet to place in her shop, and take inventory of what remains."

Her aunt's eyes widened. "Sounds as if you two accomplished quite a lot."

"We did have a little help." Grace gave her aunt a playful grin. "Aunt 'Stasia was there, too. With George. And James arrived midmorning."

"Ah, so my mischievous little sister decided to put her talents to good use instead of lurking about, attempting to find another innocent victim for her matchmaking schemes."

"Now, Auntie, you know as well as I that Aunt 'Stasia has been quite successful with her matches over the years." Grace quirked an eyebrow and gave her aunt a meaningful look. "As I recall, she was rather instrumental in arranging the match between you and Uncle Richard."

"No, as *I* recall," her aunt countered with a smile, "*you* were the key to that pairing." She replaced her teacup on her saucer and held them in her lap. "Had it not been for your insatiable love of books and your uncle's quest to assuage that love, you might never have ventured into my bookshop."

"And aren't you glad we did?"

A twinkle lit up her aunt's eyes. "Immensely so."

Grace laughed. "Still, you have to admit, your youngest sister encouraged you to pursue a dalliance with Uncle Richard." She took another small bite. "And she made certain to have a new book for me every time we came so the two of you could have uninterrupted time to talk."

Her aunt's eyes widened. "Oh, is that why you two always seemed to disappear so quickly?"

Grace winked. "We had to do something. With all the

time you spent in the bookshop, it would have been years
before a suitable gentleman captured your attention."

"And it did not harm the situation any with Anastasia being only three years your elder." She pursed her
lips and gave Grace a half grin. "The two of you could
scheme and orchestrate to your hearts' content, and you
no doubt found great pleasure in doing so."

"Well, her more so than I." Grace shrugged. "But I
enjoyed her company so much, and she made me forget
about being in that wheeled chair all day."

Aunt Charlotte nodded. "Yes, it is to Anastasia's credit
that she treats everyone equally. And with her recent en-
gagement, I am hoping to see her settle a bit in her imp-
ish ways."

"Aunt 'Stasia will always be a bit mischievous. But I
am certain George will manage to keep her somewhat
subdued from time to time." Grace grinned. "As much
as is possible, that is."

"Yes." Her aunt chuckled then gave Grace a poignant
glance. "Which brings me to the matter of *your* associations with eligible gentlemen."

Grace had wondered how long it would take her aunt
to come around to that topic. Perhaps she shouldn't have
mentioned George or James, Aunt Bethany's intended.
It was a natural segue, considering Grace remained the
only one in their family at present without a beau.

"Or lack thereof," Grace quipped.

"Yes, exactly." Her aunt took a sip of tea. "We must
do something about that."

Unbidden, Grace's thoughts wandered to Andrew, and
his face appeared before her mind's eye. She attempted to
banish him, but his roguish grin and teasing golden eyes
persisted. Why couldn't she recall his face after her ride?
When he'd been incensed. Or a few moments ago when

he'd been aloof and cordial? No, her traitorous memory would only focus on the appealing qualities and the moment when he'd been at his most charming.

"So, are you agreeable to that?" Her aunt's voice broke into her reflections.

"Pardon me?" Grace focused on her aunt. "I am sorry. I am afraid I wasn't listening."

"So I noticed." Aunt Charlotte narrowed her eyes and tilted her head just slightly. "Might something else…or perhaps *someone* else…have your attention?"

Warmth stole into Grace's cheeks and flushed her neck as well. "It is nothing."

"And that right there, young lady, is a falsehood. If you don't wish to tell me, that is fine. But do not pass it off as unimportant, when it clearly is." Her aunt's voice remained kind, yet held a distinct reprimand behind the words she spoke. "Otherwise, you would not have been so distracted as to completely miss what I said."

"You are correct, Aunt Charlotte." Grace nodded. How could she argue with such logic? "And again, I do apologize."

Her aunt brushed it off. "Never you mind. I shall find out soon enough the individual who has you slightly befuddled and not at all your usual attentive self." She paused with a wink. "In my own way."

Grace would never win that battle, so she might as well let it go. "So, what was it you said a moment ago?"

Aunt Charlotte grinned. She knew very well Grace had sidestepped the issue, but gratefully she let it drop. "I merely suggested an introduction to several young men of whom I'm aware through my association with their sisters or mothers, thanks to their patronage at the bookshop. Perhaps you would be interested in meeting them?"

"Oh! That reminds me." Grace jumped to her feet,

sloshing a few drops of her tea onto the carpet. "I must go see Uncle Richard. I have a message to deliver to him."

"Grace," her aunt chided.

Grace bent to dab a cloth onto the drops to save the parlor maids the added work. "I am sorry, Aunt Charlotte," she said as she stood once more. "I promise to return, and we can continue this discussion, but I truly must speak with Uncle Richard."

"Very well." Her aunt dismissed her. "But don't forget. We must discuss this soon."

"I won't."

Grace shoved open the doors and cringed when they slammed into their cubbies. "Sorry, Aunt Charlotte!" she called as she rushed from the room. Grace turned the corner, made her way down the hall, and had her hand on the study door when it opened without her. She braced her hands on the doorframe to keep from falling into the room.

"Oh, pardon me." Andrew paused at the doorway and stepped back inside to allow her room to enter. A second later, he shifted the rather large box he held.

She straightened and stared. Why was he here? And how had he opened the door so quickly with both hands holding what appeared to be a box of books?

"Ah, Grace," her uncle greeted. "Do come in."

So, that was how. Uncle Richard had opened it for him. That still didn't explain his presence though, or the box.

"Andrew," her uncle continued, addressing the man who regarded her with a mixture of solemnity and eagerness. "Be sure that box is delivered to Charles. He will see it's delivered to my wife's bookshop tomorrow."

Only when her uncle finished did Andrew shift his gaze from her. "Right away, Mr. Baxton."

"Well, Grace? Are you going to enter and allow Andrew to see to his work, or will you stand in the door-way until supper?"

Grace shook her head. She really needed to keep her wits about her. Stepping into the room, she made sure to give Andrew a wide berth. His eyes never left hers though as he passed to leave. And that expectant, or perhaps hopeful, look never dimmed. Did he have something to say to her? Perhaps an apology for his boorish behavior the other day? Or would it be more teasing as he'd done prior to her ride?

She certainly wouldn't find out now. Instead of say-ing anything, Andrew disappeared, leaving her staring in his wake.

Sharp snaps near her ear a moment later drew her at-tention back to her uncle. When she turned to face him, his lips curled in a bemused grin, and a twinkle lit up his eyes. Grace had to stop this. That was twice now in the span of a quarter hour when she had allowed Andrew or thoughts of him to distract her. If this persisted, someone might misinterpret her behavior and form an incorrect assumption that she found him appealing in some way.

"Uncle Richard, forgive me for interrupting your af-ternoon, but I have a message for you from James." Her aunt's intended worked at her uncle's shipyards.

"No need to apologize. What does James have to say?"

Good. Her uncle was willing to let the matter drop. "He wanted me to tell you that the shipment you were ex-pecting—the one with the coffee beans, flour, and other dry goods—arrived this morning, and he needed your signature in order to prepare it for delivery to the local shops."

"Splendid." Uncle Richard clasped his hands together and sighed. "We have been awaiting that shipment for two days now. It appears a storm set the ship slightly off course farther south down the coast. I'm pleased to see it has finally arrived." He took a couple of steps backward then turned toward his desk, where he made a brief notation on a piece of paper. "I shall make my way to the river at the first opportunity." He glanced up, one hand still resting on the desk surface. "Now, was there anything else?"

Now was as good a time as any. Grace took a step forward. "Uncle Richard?"

"Yes?"

"Did Mr. Bradenton share anything at all about his background with you?"

"Andrew?" Her uncle straightened. "Why would you ask?"

Grace wet her lips. She had to be careful not to appear too interested, or her uncle would start asking *her* probing questions. "Well, do you recall the day we went to Mr. Bancroft's shop and met Mr. Bradenton for the first time?"

She didn't know why she insisted on calling Andrew by his proper name in her uncle's presence. He referred to him as Andrew. Why shouldn't she? Distance, she told herself. She had to maintain the proper distance. And speaking his given name aloud would shatter that.

"Yes, of course," her uncle replied. "Was something amiss that day?"

"No, at least nothing beyond the obvious reason we had been called there."

She paused. How could she ask what she wanted to know without appearing inquisitive beyond cordial curiosity? In truth, she couldn't. And if she admitted it to herself, her interest extended further than mere politeness. Might as well proceed.

"I could not help but notice the clothing Mr. Bradenton wore. It did not paint him as a common thief." She gestured in the general direction of the hall. "And even now, his clothing bears distinct evidence of tailoring." Grace shrugged in an attempt to downplay her inquiry. "It does make one wonder."

Uncle Richard inhaled a deep breath and moved around his desk to perch on its edge. He folded his arms and pressed his lips into a thin line then nodded. "Yes, yes. I can see why you would ask about that. And to be honest, I don't know a lot beyond what he said to us and the judge that day. He has been quite focused on his work since his arrival."

Oh well. There went *that* chance to discover a bit more about the enigmatic addition to their household staff. Perhaps she should quit now and pursue it another time. He would be there for two and a half more months. Surely she'd learn more before he left.

"All right," she replied. "I was merely curious, and I thought you might be the best one to ask."

"Under normal circumstances, you are right. I would. But Andrew came to us as a result of a unique situation. His work has been far above standard, and I suggest we leave it at that. We know all we need to know for the time being. If he wishes to share anything further, that will be entirely up to him."

"Of course." Grace nodded, even if she was disappointed her uncle couldn't provide anything else. "And again, I am sorry for the interruption."

"Again, no apology is necessary, Grace. You are welcome to speak with me anytime."

She stepped back toward the hall and placed her hand on the doorknob. "Would you like this closed?"

"Yes, please. Thank you."

"All right. I shall see you at supper then," she called as she pulled the door shut with a click.

That conversation hadn't gone as planned, and it made her even more determined to discover something else about Andrew. She might just have to come out and ask him herself. It was the least he could do for invading her thoughts as often as he did. And there was still that matter of an apology owed to her. Grace intended to collect.

Andrew shrank back against the wall, grateful for the dimly lit hall outside Mr. Baxton's study. He prayed Grace wouldn't notice him. And he received an immediate answer to that prayer as she proceeded again toward the entryway without a backward glance or pause in her steps. He waited until she turned the corner before releasing the breath he held.

He shouldn't have been eavesdropping on her conversation with her uncle, but when he'd returned with a message from the steward and heard her still in Mr. Baxton's study, he couldn't resist. So she wanted to know more about his background. He grinned. That meant she didn't find him as offensive as she attempted to make him believe. His next breath came out somewhere between a laugh and a snort.

Now he only had to decide if he wanted to cooperate or not. The latter seemed to be the more preferable choice.

Chapter 6

The balmy breeze blew through the doorway to the kitchen, making Andrew glance in that direction as he lifted the two vats of waste. Another day, another trip to the garbage barrels. Make that four trips. He glanced over his shoulder at the cook and maids bustling about. It must be baking day the way they all scampered to and fro like mice scavenging for food. And the cook barked orders loud enough for their neighbors across the way to hear.

In this atmosphere, Andrew appreciated the opportunity to escape. Then again, perhaps he should linger a bit more until they put all the ingredients together to produce their first dessert or confection. That might make the heat of the kitchen somewhat bearable. But when he didn't continue on his way, he received a threatening glare from the cook. On second thought, perhaps not.

He steadied the containers and stepped outside. Pausing, he lifted his face to the sun. The warmth seeped into his skin. He took a deep breath then exhaled. Even the ever-present stench of the excess food in the pails he carried didn't diminish the fresh air and sense of freedom from the confines of the house. How those women survived working for hours on end in that kind of heat in their layers upon layers of clothing, he didn't know. It made him grateful for the diversity of his work.

All right, enough lollygagging. His chores wouldn't finish themselves. Andrew shifted the weight of the buckets and started forward once more. As he passed below the veranda, a slight movement captured his attention. Shifting his gaze upward, he caught sight of Miss Baxton, perched on a cushioned lounge, her mouth set in a slight grin, her eyes half-closed, and her entire demeanor quite peaceful. She held a book in front of her which, from her expression, he could only assume entertained her rather well.

Miss Baxton chose that moment to look up from her reading and over in his direction. As her gaze drifted downward, Andrew knew the moment she saw him. Her body language changed. A frown marred her lips, her eyes narrowed, and her shoulders stiffened. He offered as much of a congenial smile as he could muster. She only nodded then quickly averted her eyes.

At least she'd acknowledged him. She could have pretended she hadn't seen him at all. But as Andrew made his way to the fence, he had a sense of someone watching him. Since he hadn't noticed anyone else, it had to be Miss Baxton. A grin tugged at the corner of his mouth. Raising the buckets higher, he threw back his shoulders and marched toward the barrels. With practiced ease, he emptied the contents at the same time, silently thanking God the waste actually hit its target instead of spilling all over the ground. That would have been fitting for his foolhardy attempt at showing off. But God chose to spare him the embarrassment…this time.

Pivoting on his heel, Andrew shoved his hands into the pockets of his pants, whistled an unnamed tune, and ambled toward the veranda. He kept his gaze away from Miss Baxton as he approached, but the moment he stepped to the edge of the stone terrace, he sought her out. To the casual observer, she seemed to be absorbed in her book. But he knew better.

"Good morning, Miss Baxton."

Nothing.

Andrew cleared his throat. "Good *morning*, Miss Baxton," he repeated.

With an exaggerated sigh, she looked up from her book and made direct eye contact. "Mr. Bradenton," she replied.

She should be in the theater on stage the way she masked her interest and pretended not to notice him. Then again, he was glad she didn't sit downwind of him, or she might have to speak to him from behind a handkerchief to protect her delicate nose. He resisted the urge to take a whiff of his clothes. They couldn't possibly smell as fresh as when he'd dressed that morning. Not after that task he'd just completed. Best to keep the focus on Miss Baxton, and off of him.

Andrew nodded at the book she held. "And what is that you're reading?"

She placed a ribbon marker in the book and closed it, glancing down at the cover. "If you must know, it is Mark Twain's *The Adventures of Huckleberry Finn.*"

"Ah, yes. I read his story of Tom Sawyer a few years back. Quite a tale he tells about those boys."

Her eyes widened, and her lips parted. "You have read Mark Twain?"

He stepped onto the veranda and leaned against the railing, crossing his right ankle over his left. Andrew pretended to inspect the dirt under his fingernails and shrugged. "Of course. Why do you sound so surprised?" He pinned her with a stare. "You've read his books."

"Well, yes, but my aunt owns a bookshop, and my uncle possesses an extensive library. I do not exactly have a lack when it comes to a selection of literature with which to pass the time."

"And you don't think I also have access to a variety of books?"

"I…uh…that is…" She floundered for an appropriate response, and he forced himself not to smile. "That is not what I meant." She managed in a huff.

"So what did you mean?"

Yes, he baited her. But he couldn't resist.

Miss Baxton stuck her chin in the air just a bit but maintained eye contact. "I merely meant that I didn't expect someone like you to find books so entertaining that you would read something written by Twain."

"Someone like me?" He folded his arms across his chest. "Do you mean a thief or a servant? Or both perhaps?"

"Neither," she said without hesitation. "But rather someone who seems to prefer being out of doors instead of cooped up inside with a book."

Andrew withdrew his right hand and gestured in her direction. "You aren't inside *or* cooped up. And you're reading. There are many places where one can enjoy books."

"Point well taken."

"So I gather books are quite special to you. I've seen you in various places around the manor, seeming to enjoy the pastime."

Miss Baxton looked down at the book she held in her lap and caressed the cover. "Yes, I treasure each and every one. Have since I was a little girl." A faraway look appeared on her face. "They allow me to forget my troubles for a time and escape into another world. When I read these books, I can be anyone and go anywhere I please without concern."

Concern? Troubles? What kind of troubles could she possibly have living in a place like this, with servants tending to her every need and an uncle and aunt who doted on her like they did to their own son and daughter? For all appearances, she had everything a young lady her age could want.

"But none of these books I have are as special as the ones you stole from us and sold."

Andrew braced himself against the railing at the instant shift in her demeanor and the vengeful tone to her voice. Silent daggers shot from her eyes, and she pressed her lips into a thin line. Now how had that happened? How could she go from a melancholic state to one of anger and resentment in the span of mere seconds? And what in the world could he say in reply to that?

Choosing defeat, Andrew lowered his head and slumped his shoulders. He inhaled and released the breath slowly. "Yes, I know. And I cannot tell you how sorry I am for the distress I have caused both you and your aunt." He dared to meet her gaze again. "I wish there were some way I could make it up to you, for I know working for your uncle at the judge's orders doesn't even come close."

"No, it does not," she replied, the hard edge remaining. A moment later, she sat up straight and pressed her hands against the book in her lap, seeming to draw energy from it. "You break into our home, take what does not belong to you, and then you attempt to sell it all without any

thought to the sentimental value of the items you stole."
She paused only long enough to draw in a breath before
laying into him again. "I will have you know the books
inside that curio cabinet had been in our family for at
least six generations. One of them belonged to my aunt's
great-grandmother's great-grandmother. Aunt Charlotte
spent more than a year attempting to locate it after learning it had mistakenly been borrowed from her shop." She
looked away. "And now it's gone again, thanks to you."

Andrew couldn't be certain, but he thought he heard
a soft sniffle and could just barely see a lone tear make
its way down Miss Baxton's cheek. She kept her face
averted though. When she reached for a handkerchief
and dabbed at her nose, he knew. Andrew groaned in silence. A woman's tears were his undoing. Why did she
have to show her vulnerability? Now he'd have to do
something more to repay his debt. But what? Certainly
not say anything more that might only upset her further.

With certain defeat and as much remorse as possible
reflecting in his eyes, Andrew sighed. "Miss Baxton, I
had no idea. And you are absolutely right. I thought only
of myself and my own needs when I chose to do what I
did. It amazes me you can even tolerate my presence in
your home, much less actually acknowledge me when
our paths cross. For that, I am grateful." He pushed away
from the railing and stood tall, arms hanging straight at
his sides. "But I promise," he began, and Miss Baxton
again looked his way, "I will make it up to you."

With that, he turned and stepped off the veranda, not
even giving her a backward glance or a chance to respond. Again he felt the heat of her stare burning into his
back, but he didn't turn around. No, if he had to see her
tear-filled eyes a second longer, he might be tempted to
do something completely inappropriate. And that would

seal his fate. He was in deep enough as it was. He didn't need to complicate matters further. Distance. Distance was the key.

Grace watched Andrew walk away. So many words came to mind, and she hadn't uttered a single one. Instead, she'd chastised him and laid into him like a parent scolding a child for naughty behavior. Yes, he had caused a great deal of hurt to her and her aunt, but he had apologized, and he was serving his time, attempting to make amends. She wanted to take back her words, but it was too late.

Hadn't her aunt counseled her just that morning about the tongue being worse than a two-edged sword? Well, her sword had slashed through Andrew like the finest of sharpened steel. And that verbal wound had cut deep. His reaction made that quite clear. Grace really needed to heed her aunt's wisdom more, as well as the precepts in the scriptures. Perhaps then she wouldn't hurt Andrew again the way she just had.

Chapter 7

Grace paced back and forth in the sitting room, from the small table by the door to the fireplace against the far wall. At each turn, she stopped to rearrange the items on the table or stoke the fire. Then she crossed the room again.

"You are either going to wear that rug out clean through to the floor or you're going to put out the fire and bring a chill to this room." Aunt Charlotte spoke from her seat at the long table with Claire and Phillip, causing Grace to pause in her movements. "Or both. If you do either, you will be required to rectify it."

"I am sorry, Aunt Charlotte." Grace took a step closer to the trio. "I fear my mind is not at ease this morning, and my emotions are rather distraught."

"That much is obvious." Her aunt gave her a pointed glance. "But you are distracting your cousins from their studies. They are spending more time watching you than they are on the books in front of them."

Grace looked at Claire and Phillip, who sat sideways in their seats, their legs dangling and opposite arms draped across the backs of their chairs. Their rapt attention to her might be flattering under other circumstances. But not today.

"So," her aunt continued, "why are you remaining in this room instead of seeking out Mr. Bradenton to apologize?"

Grace snapped up her head to stare at her aunt. "How did you know?"

Charlotte pressed her lips into a thin line and tilted her head to the left, raising her eyebrows slightly. "I do have ears, my dear, and I am afraid you weren't exactly careful about how far your voice carried yesterday afternoon."

"Oh." If her aunt had heard, how many of the household staff had also been privy to that conversation? And with Andrew being one of the staff at present, if they heard her speak that way to him, would they also believe she might do the same to them?

"I can see you realize the mistake made. But what's more important is what you do about it."

"I will go find him right now."

Her aunt only nodded and said, "Very good," before returning her attention to her children.

Grace slipped from the room, careful not to distract her cousins any further. But as she stood in the foyer, she looked down the corridor toward the dining room; then she looked the other way toward her uncle's study. No sound came from either of those places, or anywhere else for that matter. Where would Andrew be at this time of day?

Well, the only way to find out would be to go searching for him. The manor wasn't too expansive, and the grounds could be covered in less than thirty minutes. Surely she'd find him somewhere. Feeling like an amateur sleuth, Grace ventured into every room she passed and peered around. Any servant in the room stopped their work and looked up when she appeared, asking if she needed anything. In light of yesterday's incident, was it any wonder? Before long they stopped asking and merely stared until she left. Oh, she had to undo the damage she'd done, and fast. Otherwise her entire relationship with the staff would be irreparably changed.

After twenty minutes only the scullery remained. Andrew couldn't possibly be in there. Could he? She'd hate to not look and later learn she'd missed him though. So she went outside to the exterior entrance and pushed open the door. Just like all the other rooms, the maids paused and looked up at her arrival. But one servant didn't.

"Mr. Bradenton!" Grace said before she could stop herself.

Andrew stopped scrubbing, but he didn't look at her. A muscle twitched in his cheek, and his breaths came slow and measured. As predicted, he remained either hurt or upset. Grace couldn't determine which. It could be both.

"Mr. Bradenton," she said again, only this time with more calm and control. "I am glad to have found you."

Still he kept his eyes downcast. Didn't he wonder why she'd sought him out? The two maids also present had no qualms about showing *their* curiosity. Not Andrew though. Grace would have preferred this conversation take place in private, but since she had yet to even garner Andrew's full attention, that possibility didn't exist. Very well. She would proceed anyway.

"You no doubt do not wish to hear from me, but I could not allow this to wait any longer."

Andrew looked as if he might actually glance up. Then, a moment later, he began scrubbing again. Perfect. Not only did he refuse to grant her eye contact, but now he had returned to his work, as if her presence didn't matter at all. He had been hurt by her words. Yes. She knew that. And she had hoped to remedy some of that now. Just not like this, feeling as if she had to work twice as hard to merely be heard. He wasn't going to make this easy. Truth be told, she likely wouldn't either, if she were in his shoes. Might as well get straight to the point.

"I confess," she continued, "this does not come easy to me, but I must beg your forgiveness for my deplorable behavior yesterday."

And still he scrubbed. Grace glanced around the serviceable room. It functioned as the location for all the washing, whether it be clothes, cooking items, or upholsteries and linens. With so much soap in great abundance, why bother scrubbing at all? Come to think of it, why was Andrew the one down on the floor? Didn't one of the maids usually do that? Could this be further punishment commanded by her uncle? Surely not. Uncle Richard wouldn't do something like that. Yet it would explain Andrew's unpleasant mood. What he did now would normally be done by a maid of the lowest ranking. No wonder he didn't want to look at her. He was no doubt embarrassed to be found in such a position.

"Mr. Bradenton…Andrew…please." Grace didn't want to beg, but she'd do what she must to be certain he heard her. "I am attempting to offer a sincere apology. The least you could do is acknowledge my presence."

Andrew mumbled something under his breath and kept moving the sudsy bristle brush back and forth across the floor.

"I beg your pardon, what did you say?"

He sighed. "It was nothing."

"It certainly did not sound like nothing to me." In fact, if she were to hazard a guess, Grace thought she heard something about maintaining dignity. She understood that in regard to his current chore, but not in regard to simple eye contact. How would looking at her be a slight against pride?

"Someone like you would never understand."

"I would like to." He seemed bound and determined to be difficult and uncooperative. And she only wanted to know why. How hard could it be to accept an apology and put it all behind him?

"No. You can't."

Grace crossed her arms. All right. Enough was enough. "I might be able to if you gave me half a chance."

She waited several moments for a reply. None came. Andrew merely remained on his knees, head bowed. Silent. Before she had a chance to say anything, the scrubbing began again. In a huff, Grace spun on her heels and left the scullery, stepping into the bright sun. Not even the harsh assault on her eyes affected her as much as Andrew's stubborn behavior. That man truly was insufferable. Well, she had said what she'd come to say. Whether he accepted her apology or not would be his choice.

Since she obviously wouldn't accomplish anything further at the house, she might as well summon Harriet and head to her aunt's bookshop. At least there she could attain a measure of success with the customers. And right now, she needed that.

"Oh, Grace. We're so glad you're here!"

Maureen fairly pounced on Grace immediately on arrival. Her longest friend, yet she lacked just a little in the area of decorum.

"Yes," Aunt 'Stasia chimed in with a grin from her position behind the front counter, "she has been waiting nearly an hour for you to arrive and talking almost as long."

"Now, that is not true, Anastasia, and you know it," Maureen countered, stomping one dainty foot. "You are just as anxious as I to hear it from Grace herself."

Grace gave them a halfhearted smile then took her time removing her wrap and hanging it on the hook by the front door. Next came her hat and gloves. Usually her aunt and friend could coax a genuine smile out of her in little or no time at all. But not today.

"All right." She made her way to the feature table near the counter and straightened a book that had been knocked over, "Now that I'm all the way inside, would one of you mind telling me what has you both so eager to speak with me?" Grace didn't exactly want to engage in a lengthy conversation, but she couldn't be rude either. "What is it you wish to hear?"

Maureen leaned forward and rested her elbows on the shelf on the other side of the counter. "First, why the long face?"

Grace picked up a random book, dusted the cover, examined the spine, and set it back down. Best to keep her response as vague as possible. She sighed. "I attempted to apologize to someone for something I said yesterday, and I'm afraid it wasn't received as well as I had hoped."

"This someone wouldn't happen to be a 'him,' would it?" Maureen nearly tipped the bookshelf in her eagerness. "Perhaps a certain new member of your servant staff?"

She should have known. In all the years she'd known Maureen, the young woman with freckles spattered across her nose had made it clear she was enamored with anything that had to do with the male species. And Aunt Charlotte had no doubt mentioned Andrew to her sisters. She shouldn't be surprised Maureen knew, too. News like that spread fast. Although it did strike her as odd that her youngest aunt wasn't more curious. She usually pounced on details such as this like a dog with a brand-new bone. Perhaps she knew more than she let on.

Grace attempted to come up with a way to share what had happened without identifying Andrew, but it was no use.

"So come on," Maureen pressed. "Don't hold back with all the details. We want to know everything!"

"Correction." Aunt 'Stasia stretched across the counter and poked Maureen with her index finger. "*You* want to know everything. I already know the basics and would be happy with just a little more."

"Oh, all right, Miss Priss." Maureen leveled a haughty glare at Anastasia. "*You* might not want to hear about this fascinating story, but *I* do." She straightened and gripped the edge of the bookshelf, barely able to contain her excitement. Her eyes held a decided gleam. A second or two later, Maureen's knuckles turned white. "Now, do tell. How did it all happen?"

So her aunt did know a little something. Grace shook her head and chuckled in spite of herself. She might not feel much like talking this morning, and the thought of time alone sounded rather appealing. Nevertheless, spending even five minutes with these two almost always bolstered her spirits.

"You don't have to share anything with her that you do not wish to share, Grace." Aunt 'Stasia narrowed her eyes at Maureen, who glared right back.

"Oh, please don't quarrel on my behalf." Grace raised her hands in a placating gesture. "I'll be more than happy to share what I can and answer any questions. I hate to disappoint you though. There truly is not much to tell."

Maureen folded her arms across her chest and stuck her chin in the air with a triumphant grin on her face. Anastasia rolled her eyes and returned her attention to the tally sheets in front of her, which marked their sales so far that day. Her aunt might appear uninterested, but Grace knew better. This was the woman who went out of her way to make matches of people who might otherwise never meet. She prided herself on seeing potential relationships where none previously existed. Between her and Maureen, Grace didn't stand a chance.

She picked up an apple from the basket on the counter and took a bite, savoring the sweet juices. After swallowing, she shifted to lean against the table behind her and settled back to describe her encounters with Mr. Andrew Bradenton. From their first meeting to the handful of brief conversations that followed, Grace shared enough to cover the essentials and ended with the episode from earlier that morning, but kept her retelling strictly factual. No sense borrowing trouble just yet. That would come soon enough, especially with these ladies involved.

"I can scarcely fathom having someone like him working under the very same roof where I sleep at night," Maureen remarked when Grace finished. "And the times your paths have crossed. I'm amazed you haven't done everything you could to avoid him." She took a step forward and rested one arm on the counter. "I know I would."

"Well, I can't exactly make it obvious that I don't wish to be in the same room with him," Grace replied, even if her words were far from the truth.

"Still…" Maureen's eyes lit up again, a sure sign of trouble. "There is a certain appeal to the knowledge that this Mr. Bradenton is being forced to work for your family to repay his debt. Then there is the matter of his obvious class position and tailored clothing. From the way you talk about him, I gather he is quite handsome, too."

And her friend had returned. The fanciful, daydreaming, obsessed-with-stories-of-romance friend. She could be rather trying at times, and her constant focus on the potential for amorous associations might be bothersome to most. But Grace wouldn't have it any other way.

Aunt 'Stasia waved her hand to get Grace's attention. "So will you attempt to speak with him again? Perhaps to be sure he accepts your apology?"

"I don't know." Grace twisted the apple she held and watched the light reflect off its shiny skin. "I suppose I should, if for no other reason than to be certain any harm done is repaired."

"Oh yes," Maureen added. "Don't even consider the possibility that he might be the prince of your dreams or something remotely similar, Miss Practical." Maureen waved her hand in dismissal as she straightened and picked up a stack of books in need of shelving. "Do me a favor though. If you spoil your chances with this gentleman, please cease from informing me about it. I only wish to hear a report of your time with him if the discussions go well."

Aunt 'Stasia shuffled a few steps to her left and leaned over the counter toward Grace. "Pay her no mind. You do what you feel you have to do." She reached out and placed a reassuring hand on Grace's arm. "And regardless of whether or not Maureen wishes to hear of your future encounters with this gentleman, you can always come find me if you're in need of someone to listen."

Grace gave her aunt an appreciative smile. "Thank you. I will be certain to tell you both what happens." She glanced at the large clock on the wall. "Now, we should all get some work done before the day disappears without us."

Once settled into the routine tasks at the bookshop, Grace couldn't get her mind off Andrew. She had managed to push him somewhat to the back of her mind on the carriage ride to the shop, but thanks to Maureen's romantic fantasies, Andrew now occupied her thoughts fully. What was she going to do? Both her friend and her aunt would be sure to follow up on this presumed or potential relationship. And they would want to know more about Andrew's background. But how would she find out something like that? She couldn't just walk up to him and ask him about it.

Then again, why couldn't she?

Chapter 8

"You are coming to the shipping office and docks today, Andrew." Mr. Baxton's no-nonsense voice sounded from the other side of the door Andrew was repairing. "Meet me in the front hall at half past eight."

Andrew leaned back on his haunches to peer around the door, but Baxton had disappeared. The man didn't leave any room for a response. Then again, since he had issued a command and not a request, a reply wouldn't be necessary. At least not one he would expect, anyway.

So the shipyard would be his destination today. Andrew resumed tightening the hinges and pictured it all in his mind. He had traveled the Delaware River a handful of times on business for the mill, but most of his work ended up with him holding the reins and driving a cart or wagon full of supplies. Once in a while, he ventured to Baltimore or Philadelphia via train. But the main port in Wilmington? The grand ships, the merchant tradesmen, the sailors. So many different people coming and going. He could hardly wait to leave.

A glance over his shoulder at the clock on the wall showed he had forty minutes until the instructed meeting time. Might as well finish the door and maybe get the repairs finished on that bench in the hall. He'd have to meet Mr. Baxton there. Early would be best. And if he was there, that wouldn't be a problem.

Thirty-five minutes later, Mr. Baxton came into the front hall from his study. "Ah, good. You're here already. Excellent." He nodded to Harrison, who held out his coat and top hat. "Shall we go then?"

"I'm ready."

"I have already called for the carriage, sir," Harrison said in his drone voice. "It should be waiting outside momentarily."

"Thank you, Harrison."

Like his niece, Baxton gave the butler direct eye contact, not merely the cursory nod. It said so much about the man and his relationship with those who served him. Harrison opened the door for them both, and as Andrew passed the butler, he looked him straight in the eye.

"Thank you," Andrew said with a nod.

Harrison didn't reply, but Andrew didn't expect a response. The butler did show a minor reaction in his eyes though. Just enough for Andrew to know his actions had an effect. Technically, he ranked lower than the butler, but that wouldn't be forever. This could be a new way of handling things, and it could make quite a difference with the servants at his father's home. Yes. He would do it. He would make the effort to treat them all better, no matter their station.

Once settled inside the carriage, Andrew admired the plush seats and custom craftsmanship on the interior. In fact, it looked rather familiar. He glanced at the small plate just below the window in the door. Gregg & Bowe Fine Carriages. A rather prominent Philadelphia company that had expanded down to Wilmington as well. Yes, he thought he recognized their work. His own father used the same company.

Baxton plopped his top hat on the seat beside him, flipped open the day's issue of *The Morning News*, and settled back against his seat. Andrew supposed he should do the same, but he couldn't relax. What had made Baxton change his mind all of a sudden and assign him somewhere other than the manor? And would it be the same as his work so far? Emptying waste, scrubbing, and doing minor repairs?

Andrew looked across at Baxton. Engrossed in the paper, the man didn't look like he'd be talking anytime soon. That left the passing scenery to occupy Andrew's attention as they traveled to the southeast, toward the river junctures. And that meant it would be a long ride.

Without even glancing up from whatever he read, Baxton suddenly folded the paper and tucked it under his arm. A few seconds later, the carriage slowed and came to a stop.

"We are here," was all Baxton said before stooping to exit the carriage.

How had he known if he hadn't been paying attention or watching the landmarks they'd passed as Andrew had done? Sure, he no doubt traveled this route often, but no one could know a path that well, could they? Amazing.

The faint brackish air and the smell of marshland hit Andrew's nose. Why hadn't he smelled that until now? He'd been watching out the window the entire time. They didn't live too far from the river, but the slight change of scenery from the residential and business district to the waterways was usually hard to miss. His mind was definitely somewhere else.

Left with no other choice but to follow in Baxton's wake, Andrew stepped down from the carriage and rushed along the uneven cobblestones to walk just a step behind him. A few seagulls let loose with their distinct calls, and the faint sound of water lapping at the shore reached his ears. After about a minute Baxton spoke again.

"You no doubt are wondering why I've brought you here today."

Yes, that was exactly what Andrew wanted to know.

"Well, it has been one month since you started working for us, and I figured it was about time to give you a more meaningful task." Baxton glanced over his shoulder with a pointed stare. "Mind you, I did not have to do this. You know as well as I that the judge left the specifics of your sentencing up to my discretion."

How well Andrew knew that. He had to remind himself of it almost every day, but especially when his tasks bordered on something a young page could do.

"But," Baxton continued, facing forward again and never once breaking his stride, "you have demonstrated exemplary dedication and thoroughness in everything you have done, no matter the work. Do not think it has gone unnoticed." He clasped his hands behind his back. "For that, I am grateful." Then he unclasped them and slowed his stride.

Andrew eased his pace as well, careful not to walk ahead. He didn't know where he was going anyway, so he *had* to follow Baxton.

"Mrs. Baxton and I have spoken at length about this, and she agrees with my decision. We both feel you should have the opportunity to work here at the shipyard as well.

Being cooped up inside so long isn't good for a man, particularly one who is no stranger to the out-of-doors."

Well, Baxton had that part right. Andrew had spent a great deal of time working in the sun at the mill. His skin no doubt showed that. And unlike the genteel ladies around him, the telltale marks of sun weren't a definitive sign of the lower classes. Not that it mattered to Baxton. Andrew was still a servant, and who he was before he stole was inconsequential.

"With that being said"—Baxton paused and swept his left arm outward in an arc—"I give you Hannsen & Baxton Shipping."

Andrew stepped forward to be even with the brick archway covering the path where they stood. His eyes widened. Laid out before him stood an impressive sentinel of ships of varying lengths and designs. Several barques, a handful of clippers, a flyboat or two, a collier, three fishing smacks, some schooners and brigantines, a windjammer, and a trawler. Andrew clenched and unclenched his fists. He leaned forward on his toes and rocked back on his heels. His breaths came in shorter spurts.

Baxton chuckled. "I see you are a man after my own heart." He clapped Andrew on the back. "So I was not mistaken in my estimation of your interests. You will do much better here than at the manor." With a random wave of his hand, he added, "The work you've been doing is better left to the household staff anyway. You? I have far more challenging tasks in mind."

Andrew didn't know if that should excite or concern him. For now, he'd tread lightly...at least until he knew for certain what Baxton would have him do.

"So," Baxton said as he clapped his hands and held them together, "shall we get started?"

Andrew shrugged. "I'm at your service, sir."

"Very well. We shall begin at the main office here in port."

With that, Baxton led the way to a nondescript brick building with the company's name emblazoned on a shingle hanging over the main door. It sat just to the left of a larger three-story brick building with the same name on a large metal plate near the roof. That must be where the smaller manufacturing work took place. Once inside, the layout and overall appearance reminded Andrew of his father's mill office farther up the Brandywine. As Baxton explained the roles of each person working in the office, Andrew's mind drifted.

"You will be overseeing the staff here in the office," his father had told him the day he'd promoted him to a supervisory role. "Choose each individual carefully. It's essential to have a team whose strengths and weaknesses complement each other. Otherwise, the efficiency is at risk and so is the productivity."

And Andrew had done just that. It had meant reassigning two workers to other areas of the mill, but the end result far outweighed the brief bump in the road of adjustment to the new order of things. Now, as he listened to Baxton report on the operation of the shipping office, Andrew realized this man and his partners utilized a similar practice.

"This shipping company has been in my family for well over one hundred years. We are second only to Harlan & Hollingsworth Company, with J. A. Harris Shipyard running a close third to our industry's output. Mrs. Baxton's family has a similar lineage going back six generations. One of her great-grandfathers was in the British Royal Navy." He smiled, more to himself than at Andrew. "I, too, have direct ties to Britain. We are grateful our ancestors eventually switched their allegiance to the Patriots, or this company might not exist today."

"I can well understand that," Andrew replied. "For a company thriving on trade and industry, loyalty to the United States would have been essential, especially once the British pulled out their support. Now it's not such a significant element, but following the War for Independence, it would have been critical."

"Exactly." Baxton nodded, seemingly impressed with his response. "We merged with my wife's family company about four years ago. It's been quite the experience getting operations running smoothly and adjusting to the new branches of shipbuilding and manufacturing."

"I can imagine." So that explained how the company increased its holdings so fast. He'd heard reports but hadn't been involved in business and trade as extensively in recent months.

"It's a good thing the visions of the two companies aligned," Baxton continued, "or the merger might not have been successful."

"Yes. My father owns Diamond State Mills, and he merged with another mill not long ago to acquire the manufacturing of jute, yarns, and twine, in addition to the rifle powder and millinery supplies they specialized in up to that point." Andrew wasn't sure how much to reveal, but Baxton no doubt knew of his family at this point anyway. He didn't get to be in charge of a successful shipping company without connections and knowledge. "Stepping into unfamiliar territory is always an adjustment. You have to love what you do and respect your employees to make it work."

"Let us just say," Baxton said as they paused by a rear door, "shipping seems to be in our blood, flowing strong and vital. Even as a new era dawns with the increased appearance of steamships and iron hulls, we will remain dedicated to keeping our company thriving, no matter the cost."

Andrew didn't have anything to say to that. He didn't feel it was his place either. For some reason, Mr. Baxton had decided to provide him with a great deal of background information that didn't seem necessary. They ambled down toward the river's edge, where a flurry of activity could be seen on board several of the ships. With them docked, the normal crew wouldn't be present. But the skeleton crews who made certain the ships stayed in excellent condition would always be there. Baxton's ships stood like beacons in port, beckoning to all who gazed on them and signaling that the owners took great pride in their property.

Shouts rang out, commands floated on the air, and the few crew members on deck scrambled to heed the orders. Every man knew his duty, and he did it without complaint. In fact, they seemed to thrill to the task. Was it any wonder? Men didn't sign up to work on board a ship if they didn't love it. Andrew gazed up as they came to the river's edge. He shaded his eyes from the morning sun, now about midway in the eastern sky. Seagull screeches fused with human voices in a cacophony of sounds. The port was alive with activity, and Andrew could hardly wait to get started.

"As you can see"—Baxton again reined in Andrew's focus—"we keep most of our ships here near the mouth of the Christina. But some of them are docked across the way at Helms Cove." He pointed through the narrow view between two ships.

Although the width of the Delaware River made it impossible to see clearly to the other side, Andrew knew of the cove. He'd been on a ship once that had sailed from there farther south down the river toward the bay and ocean.

Baxton signaled to a man who had just come down off one of the ships and now headed their way. "I would like to introduce you to the man who will be overseeing your work here with the ships."

When the man stood a yard away, Baxton made the introductions.

"James Woodruff, I'd like you to meet Andrew Bradenton." Baxton turned his shoulders to include Andrew, but he didn't look at him. Instead, he kept his eyes focused on James. "Andrew, this is James. Should you have any questions at all, or should you need to report the completion of a task, you are to come see him."

James extended a hand. "Mr. Baxton has already told me about you. I'm looking forward to seeing what you can do with some of these beauties."

Andrew hesitated a fraction of a second before he took the proffered hand and gave it a firm shake. "And I'm looking forward to the challenge."

Preston held his gaze a moment longer than what Andrew felt necessary, and if he read it right, there was a distinct narrowing of the eyes coupled with a silent animosity, although on a minimal level. Not that he hadn't grown accustomed to looks like that in the month he'd been serving his sentence. He *was* a thief after all, and that invariably caused suspicion in anyone who met him for the first time, especially if his crime had preceded that introduction.

Still, if Baxton could trust him enough to tend to his ships, the man must have seen something worthwhile. Andrew didn't know how to deal with that though. He could handle being treated like the criminal he now was. But his benefactor had deemed him ready for something more. That alone made him determined to avoid making a mistake…any mistake…that might send him back to the manor. Then again, a rather charming young lady remained back there. And that put him in a quandary.

Accept the tasks Baxton had for him here at the shipyard and surrender the chance of crossing paths with Miss Baxton, or return to the manor and the mundane work of household staff simply to be near her. Andrew couldn't decide which held greater appeal.

Chapter 9

Grace perched on the edge of the seat cushion inside the carriage. She shifted back and forth to get a good view out the side window. The briny air coupled with the faint call of seagulls and geese started her legs bouncing and her feet tapping on the carriage's floor. Harriet sat calmly on the seat opposite her. How could she not be affected? After being confined to the manor more this past winter than at any other time of year, Grace wanted to jump out right now and run the rest of the way. But she wouldn't. Someone might see her. What would people think?

And what if Andrew happened to be here? She didn't want to admit that possibility was half of her reason for telling her aunt she'd come today. He'd been gone from the manor for less than three days, yet despite his boorish behavior when last they spoke, Grace missed seeing him. If he was somewhere visible, she didn't need to make a fool of herself.

The *clip-clop* of the horses' hooves slowed to a dirge-like pace. How much farther? Had this part of the journey always taken this long? Grace peered out the window again, attempting to determine the reason for the delay. A rather angry pair of voices reached her ears a moment later.

"This is entirely your fault," one voice stated, his words punctuated with annoyance. "And don't try to tell me otherwise."

"My fault?" the other voice replied. "This wouldn't have happened if you had been more careful with that oversized wagon of yours."

"And my wagon wouldn't have been in your way if you had taken the path meant for carts like yours." Grace saw an arm extend into her view as one of the men pointed. "Over there. On the other side of the stone wall."

"I have a right to be here, same as you or anyone else," the second man said.

"Yes," the first man replied, "but you don't have a right to protest or complain when a wagon upsets your cart because you were driving it on the path meant for larger delivery wagons."

Grace scooted closer to the door and stuck her head out the window. Her driver turned in his seat to look back at her.

"We shall be through this in just a few minutes, Miss Baxton. I am sorry for the delay."

She waved off his apology. "No worries, Matthew. You could not possibly have foreseen this happening." And unfortunately, neither could she, or she *would* have jumped out of the carriage much sooner. Now she could only wait.

"We aren't going to get anywhere arguing over who was at fault more," the second voice continued. "But could you at least help me get my cart right side up again so I can put my fruits and vegetables back in it?"

"Why should I help you? I wasn't in the wrong here."

Grace could imagine the first man standing there, arms crossed, looking down his nose at the other man. She hadn't seen the accident, but from the sounds of things, the second man shouldn't have been there. Still, the first likely could have avoided it if he had been more careful with his driving. So, in a way, they were both to blame. And that meant both should set the cart right once more.

"You're just going to stand there and watch?" the second man asked.

"Seems like a good idea to me," the first replied.

Grace had had enough. They would get nowhere at this rate. And that river beyond beckoned to her. She turned the handle to the door and pushed it open. Gathering her skirts close, she placed one foot on the step and descended from the carriage. Heedless of propriety or her uncle's standing caution to remain in the carriage until the footman deemed it safe for her, Grace marched right up to the two men. She stepped around scattered oranges, apples, broccoli spears, and heads of lettuce in her path.

The two men halted their argument when she came into view and turned to stare. They looked her up and down, and one man ran his beefy hand across the two days' growth on his jaw. A lascivious look entered his eyes. Grace forced back a shiver. Based on where he stood, that had to be the first man she'd heard, the one who refused to help in any way.

"Pardon me, but would it be possible for you two gentlemen to remedy this situation at a speedier pace? I have a message to deliver to my uncle, and my driver and I need to pass."

"Need to see your uncle, do you?" He raised his eyebrows, and his tongue snaked out to wet his lips. "Maybe we can escort you to him then. It wouldn't take long."

"Aw, come on, Jensen. Leave the lady be, will you? She's only trying to get to where she's going."

The smaller man wore an apron over his clothes, and his shirtsleeves were rolled to his elbows. His receding hairline and bushy eyebrows reminded her of the butcher near her aunt's bookshop. At least Grace didn't have to deal with two ill-mannered men.

The man called Jensen whipped around to face the other man. "You shut your mouth, Lucas." He slowly turned back to Grace. "I'm only trying to be…hospitable…to the lady."

He'd had to search for *that* word. Under normal circumstances, his attempt at more refined speech would have made Grace smile. But his uncouth behavior ruled that out.

"Well, she doesn't need your hospitality," Lucas retorted. "She needs to see her uncle. And if you would help me, we could get this mess cleaned up so she could be on her way."

"I'll even give you a hand."

Grace jumped a little at Matthew's voice coming from just over her right shoulder. She hadn't even heard him jump down from his perch in front of the carriage. The two men also regarded him with instant wariness.

"Miss Baxton," Matthew said, lightly touching her arm, "why don't you wait in the carriage. I promise we'll have this all cleared away in a jiffy."

Jensen and Lucas looked back and forth from Matthew to Grace. A small smile tugged at the corner of her lips. Jensen's demeanor had changed the second he'd noticed Matthew. And for good reason, too. Her driver wasn't

exactly lacking in size, and he could present an impos-
ing presence when he so desired. Grace turned to leave
but paused when Jensen inhaled a sharp breath and his
eyes widened.

"Wait a minute," he said, holding up his right hand in a
staying gesture. "Did you say Baxton? As in Hannsen &
Baxton Shipping right here at the river?" He swallowed
slowly, his Adam's apple bobbing once. "So your uncle
is Richard Baxton?"

"Yes," Grace replied. "Yes, he is."

Jensen straightened and immediately spun toward the
upset cart. "I am terribly sorry, miss. Forgive us for keeping you from your business." He grabbed hold of the cart
and, with Matthew's help, set it right once more. Then
he reached for whatever items he could find near his feet
and dumped them in the back of the cart.

Lucas stood watching, his mouth open. Matthew took
a step back and waited near the horses. A few seconds
later, Lucas stooped to retrieve his goods from the ground
around his own feet. But Jensen worked much faster. In
less than two minutes, the obstruction had been cleared
and all items returned to the cart.

Jensen approached and paused in front of Grace. With
a slight bow, he also lowered his head. "Again, please
forgive the delay. I was on my way to Baxton's shipyard
when this whole accident happened." He made direct
eye contact once more, all evidence of carnal thought
eradicated from his expression. In its place, only veiled
respect remained. "If I can help in any other way, I will
be happy to do so."

The man's instant change in demeanor surprised
Grace. He obviously knew her uncle, or at least knew
of him, enough so that the mere mention of her uncle's
name sent the man into immediate obedience. It hap-

pened often, especially here at the shipyard. But that didn't make Jensen's behavior any less inappropriate, simply because he'd tried to save face the moment he'd heard the name Baxton. Nevertheless, it wasn't her place to chastise him for it.

"Thank you, Mr. Jensen." Grace held out her hand, and Jensen accepted it briefly with another bow. "But that will not be necessary. I appreciate your offer though. Thank you for resolving this state of disorder so promptly."

"My pleasure, miss," Jensen replied, taking a step back.

"Have a nice day, Miss Baxton," Lucas called, his hand raised with two fingers and a thumb up in a minor wave.

Grace nodded. "Matthew," she called over her shoulder, "I believe I'm ready to finish the drive to our destination now."

Beyond ready, actually. Grace returned to the carriage and accepted Matthew's assistance inside. If Jensen thought enough of her uncle to change his actions so abruptly, Uncle Richard should know about the incident. It might change his dealings with Jensen, or at the very least make him speak to the man.

A few short minutes later, Matthew stopped the carriage again and hopped down to help Grace out.

"Thank you," she said and waited for him to close the door. "I shouldn't be too long inside, but if that changes, I will be sure to send someone out to notify you."

"Very good, miss," Matthew replied. He moved to stand next to the horses then stretched his arms overhead and brought them down to twist to the left and right.

Grace rolled her shoulders a little, feeling the slight stiffness from the ride. She didn't have the luxury of working out the kinks though. Not here in public anyway. Perhaps the walk along the river to her uncle's office would ease the aches.

She made her way down the cobblestone path toward the brick archway that served as a gateway of sorts to the riverfront. She stood under the arch and breathed in the distinct pungent scent of the river. Grace always thrilled to the unique aroma. It didn't possess the same appeal as the salty sea air of the ocean farther south, but it held its own regardless. With the abundance of bass, herring, carp, and trout, along with the various waterfowl feeding on those fish, and the constant movement of the shipyards or merchant trade, the river never lacked for activity. Compared to life at the manor, the river teemed with excitement.

"Hey! Bradenton!" A voice boomed down a few hundred feet from where Grace stood, and she looked that direction. "Get that sail secured then come help me sift this powder and clean out the cannons."

Grace shielded her eyes and scanned the ships for sight of Andrew. Her eyes hopped from person to person working on board the ships until she finally spotted Andrew's familiar form two ships away. He had just lowered the main sail and now rolled it on top of the boom. Like all the other workers and sailors, he wore a pullover cotton shirt with dropped shoulders and full sleeves to allow for freedom of movement. The cream color suited his skin tone, and it was tucked into a pair of beige canvas trousers, held up with a set of Y-back braces. His gray wool tweed cap reminded Grace of Jesse from their stables. Andrew sure knew how to blend in with everyone. And he did it quite well.

The piercing *cheereek* of an osprey leaving its nest and taking to flight drew Grace's attention overhead. The brownish-black raptor spread its impressive wings and flew over the ships toward the river, its keen eyes scouting the water for a fresh catch. As soon as it disappeared from her sight, Grace returned her attention to the ship where Andrew worked.

Even from this distance, she took note of his broad shoulders and the way his muscles flexed as he tied the knot around the sail and boom. He cut a rather impressive figure, and warmth crept into Grace's cheeks at her scandalous appraisal. What would her aunt say if she were here to witness her niece behaving in such a manner?

"Bradenton! Let's get moving. The day won't wait forever."

That same booming voice called out, and Andrew finished securing his knot with a deft yank. He stood and stretched, much like Matthew had, only Grace found Andrew's actions far more compelling.

"On my way!" Andrew called in return. Then, as if he sensed her staring, he turned and looked right at her.

Grace startled, but she couldn't look away. Heat raced up her neck and lapped at her cheeks. Despite the expanse of space between them, his gaze held her captive. A slow smile spread across his lips. At closer proximity, Grace was certain a distinct twinkle would be in his eyes as well. She had to break the trance. Somehow. But her body refused to cooperate. Then he raised a hand to wave, and she shook free from the invisible ties.

Away. She must get away. Ah, yes. Her uncle's office. She had a message for him. The perfect excuse to flee from this embarrassing moment. With haste, she spun on her heel, stumbling and catching herself before she fell. Grace dared not look back over her shoulder for fear that Andrew might still be watching.

"Ah, Grace." Uncle Richard looked up from the desk

where he leaned, going over some papers his reception-ist held. "What brings you to the office today?"

Good. She didn't have to wait to see to her main purpose for this visit. Waiting would only leave her mind to wander to Andrew and the incident from a moment ago.

"I have a message from Aunt Charlotte." Grace reached into her reticule to retrieve the folded note. "She said she didn't need a response until you returned home this evening."

Her uncle reached out for the note. "Very good. Thank you."

Grace looked around the front room of the office. Nothing had changed since last autumn, not even the staff who worked there. And there was something comforting in the familiar. The familiar didn't come with any surprises, and it certainly didn't cause any embarrassing situations.

Just then the door opened and in walked Andrew. Grace averted her eyes and focused first on the sofas and chairs nearby, then on the scenic painting hanging over the waiting area. Anywhere but at the man who'd made fiery heat a consistent temperature on her face three times already that day.

"Andrew." Uncle Richard acknowledged his entrance. "Finished with the cannons already?"

"No, sir," Andrew replied, and Grace glanced at him from the corner of her eye. "We will likely be working on those most of the afternoon. Sifting the powder, too." He stepped closer. "I have a progress update from James though. He asked me to bring it directly to you." Andrew reached into the patch pocket on his shirt and handed the note to Uncle Richard.

"So," her uncle said as he took the note and read the scribbled words, "It appears you're having a rather successful day thus far. Impressive." He nodded. "I appreciate the report. Seems the good weather has been in your favor."

"Yes. The clear blue skies and minimal wind have made securing sails and airing out the gunpowder a rather simple feat." He turned his head to look in her direction. "And the view is undeniably riveting."

For a fourth time her cheeks flamed, and Grace jerked her face away from anyone who might see her. This had to stop. Someone might think she was ill with the constant flush.

"I won't argue with you there," her uncle replied, completely oblivious to Andrew's concealed reference to her staring. "It's impressive from the ground, but from the deck of a ship? Thrilling!"

"Well, I had best get back to work or they might wonder about the delay in my return. Good day, sir." Again Grace peered at him. Andrew bowed to her uncle and turned toward her. "Miss Baxton." His voice held a hint of mirth as he tipped his cap in her direction. "Always a pleasure."

And with that he was gone. The door clicked closed behind him, leaving Grace to stare at the space he'd just occupied. She swallowed several times and wet her lips, praying her face had returned to some semblance of a normal color. Good thing Andrew hadn't engaged her beyond those few words. She likely wouldn't have been able to produce a reply. At least not one that would make any sense. And she didn't babble. Not for any reason or anyone.

"Grace," her uncle asked, "are you going to stand there and stare at the door all afternoon, or was there some other reason you've come here today?"

Grace spun to face her uncle. "No, Uncle Richard. I

only came to give you Aunt Charlotte's note. I've done that. So now I believe I will take a walk along the river."

He nodded. "Just be sure Harriet remains with you at all times." Her uncle signaled to one of his clerks. "And I shall alert James to your intentions, so he can keep a watchful eye as well. You can never be too careful."

"Thank you, Uncle." Grace didn't relish the thought of having more than one chaperone, but her uncle was right. After the encounter she'd had prior to her arrival, she must remain cautious. She started to head for the door then stopped with her hand on the knob. "Oh! Uncle Richard. I almost forgot." She turned to face him again.

"Yes?"

"There was a man I met on my way here, just before Matthew dropped off Harriet and me at the walkway. Some altercation involving a wagon and a cart. But the man's name was Jensen, and he said he was on his way to meet you."

"Jensen? Yes, I know of him." Her uncle gave her his undivided attention. "What about him?"

How would she tell this without implicating herself too much? "Well, he wasn't the most mannerly of men upon first introductions. But when he learned who I was…or more importantly who *you* were, his entire demeanor changed." Grace shrugged. "I thought you would like to know."

Uncle Richard narrowed his eyes and peered at her for several moments, as if weighing the truth of her story. "We'll speak on this more when I return home this evening. I have a feeling there is more than you are telling me. But thank you for what you *have* said." He nodded toward the door. "Now, I believe you have a walk to take?"

Grace said her good-byes and left the office. Harriet hung back several paces, close enough to be there if needed but far enough away to give Grace some privacy. And she desperately needed it. Her thoughts had remained on Andrew the entire time she'd stood in her uncle's office. Now that she walked alone, the memory of Andrew catching her staring returned full force.

Just a few days ago, he'd been less than cordial, bordering on impolite. Today he'd had the audacity to grin like a rake at her and even make a veiled reference to the incident in her uncle's presence. Then there was the twinkle in his eye as he'd tipped his hat and left. It was enough to drive her mad. Grace inhaled the familiar scents of the river, already relishing the invigorating breaths she could take. Yes, this walk would do her a world of good toward clearing her head.

Chapter 10

"Grace?"

Uncle Richard called to her from his office, so she filed the current folder she held, shut the drawer, and stepped into the other room.

"Yes, sir?"

"Would you do me a favor?" He consulted a spreadsheet of sorts on the desk in front of him, but she couldn't make out the heading at the top. A second later, he looked up at her. "Would you walk down to the ships and fetch Andrew for me? Tell him I need to speak with him as soon as he's available."

"You wish Andrew to come here? Why not speak with him down at the dock?" This had to be something of great import. She hoped he hadn't done anything to upset her uncle.

"Because what I have to say to him is best said without other listening ears."

Grace tilted her head just a little to the right. Her uncle didn't give an indication if the upcoming conversation would be serious or a run-of-the-mill topic. And it wasn't her place to ask. That didn't stop the questions though. Why didn't he want anyone else to overhear him? How would here at his office be any different than his study at home? Or even in the carriage ride home, since Andrew rode with him each day? Both of those would afford him the privacy he sought. And what made him ask *her* to go find Andrew? Why not one of his clerks?

"I would like to speak with him sooner rather than later, Grace." His voice held a hint of amusement.

"Oh!" She shook her head. Best to not ruminate too much with her uncle watching. "I am sorry, Uncle Richard." She placed one hand on the doorframe. "I will go straightaway to find him for you."

"Thank you."

He returned his attention to the spreadsheet in front of him, picking up a pencil to make some additional notations. Grace turned in a slow arc. She wouldn't get anything further from her uncle at this point. Perhaps afterward he would be more inclined to answer some of her questions…at least the ones she'd be permitted to ask.

"Harriet, I'll only be a few minutes," she said to her maid who rose from her seat. "No need for you to join me."

Grace grabbed her satin bonnet from the coatrack by the door and looped the ties beneath her chin as she stepped outside. She squinted and blinked a few times as her eyes adjusted to the bright light of the sun. If she could, she'd be outside more often. She walked down the path toward the docks. Aunt Charlotte would never approve of so much time spent being exposed to the sun. Grace touched the chiffon ties, wishing she could have

left the bonnet inside. From what her uncle told her, she'd
inherited her mother's wanderlust spirit. Her father had
been content to remain cooped up behind a desk. But
not her mother, and not her uncle. And certainly not her.

"Afternoon, Miss Grace." One of the swabbies tipped
his hat to her as she passed.

"Good afternoon, Henry." She smiled at one of the few
crewmen she knew by name, a man whose wife would be
delivering a new baby any day now. "Are you and Clara
still praying for a little boy?"

"Yes'm, we are." He leaned on the pole end of the mop
he held and grinned. "With them three girls we got, it'd
be nice to have a boy to give them what for and help me
keep them in line." Henry swayed a little closer to her.
"And I wouldn't mind learning him a trade right here
with the ships neither."

"No, I do not imagine you would." Grace nodded.
"Passing on a legacy is a fine and admirable dream,
Henry. You keep praying. I know the Lord is listening."

"Yes'm. I know He is, too." He straightened and assumed a more down-to-business expression. "Now, is
you here for a walk, or do you gots business from Mr.
Baxton?"

Ah, good. She might save some time if Henry could
assist her. "Actually, Henry, I am on an errand for my
uncle. He needs to speak to Mr. Bradenton as soon as
possible. Might you know where I could locate him?"

"Sure do." He pointed. "He be down there on that collier yonder, about five docks down."

Grace looked in the direction he'd indicated. She
couldn't make out any individual worker from this distance, but if Henry saw him there, Andrew would be
there.

"Thank you, Henry. You have saved me a great deal of time."

Henry tipped his rather worn slouch hat. "My pleasure, Miss Grace."

She took a few steps toward the collier then heard Henry call out to her.

"I'll be sure and tell you bouts the baby when he or she gets here."

Grace raised one hand in acknowledgment and continued walking. She glanced up at each ship she passed. As usual, the smaller crew retained while the ships were in port all bustled about, seeing to their duties. It never ceased to amaze her that a single ship would require so much work when it wasn't even sailing. But her uncle had told her about the need for keeping the deck swabbed, the cabins below free of moisture, rats, and other vermin, and the anchor free of barnacles. Then they had to check the tackle, repair the cables, examine the rigging, and tend to any necessary repairs on board to make certain the ship continued to be seaworthy. No wonder some men could say they spent every day of the year on board a ship.

And no wonder her uncle had employed Andrew here at the shipyard rather than back at the manor. His skills seemed far more suited to this work than the everyday tasks back home. It took a lot of work to maintain her uncle's impressive fleet, and Uncle Richard no doubt capitalized on Andrew's sentence and his strength to benefit the most from both.

Grace stopped at the ship she hoped was the collier Henry had pointed out. Yes. No doubt about it. She'd found the right ship. Blackened sails from the coal dust, no ornamentation, and no figurehead. She could only imagine the travails of sailing on such a vessel. When she sailed, she primarily spent her time on board the *Am-*

ethyst, one of her uncle's merchant ships. This ship spent most of its time sailing the Chesapeake and transporting the coal from the Virginia mines. Cleaning it would take days. And how could the crewmen ever keep from getting the dust all over them?

She looked up to the bow of the ship and had the answer. They didn't. A giggle escaped her lips, and she covered her mouth with her hand. Andrew dumped a bucket of black water over the port bow then raised one arm to swipe it across his forehead, smearing the layer of grime and dust and leaving a track where his sleeve had touched. With the sun beating down from overhead, the heat likely made the working conditions quite unpleasant. But Andrew presented such a comical image, Grace couldn't hold back the laughter.

Andrew paused midway to bringing the bucket back over the rail and looked down. When he spotted her, he grinned, his teeth standing out even more in the middle of a blackened face.

"I have a message for you," she called, raising her voice just enough to be heard but not enough to draw unwanted attention.

He signaled for her to wait, and a moment later, he made his way toward the gangplank leading from the ship to the dock. Andrew jogged down it and leaped the remaining distance when he had almost reached the end. In no time at all, he stood opposite her, coal dust covering every visible part of him.

Again laughter bubbled up from within, and she tried to stifle it. No such luck. She covered her mouth a second time, her shoulders shaking from the mirth.

"Do tell, Miss Baxton, what you find so amusing?"

He no doubt hadn't the faintest idea what he looked like. A looking glass wouldn't be of great concern on board a ship, and certainly not for the workers. But someone should tell him, and since he asked, it would have to be her.

Grace removed her hand from her mouth and lowered her arm to her side. "Please forgive me, Mr. Bradenton, but your face. And your clothes." She pressed her lips together to stave off another chuckle. "They're black."

As if it had just dawned on him how he might appear to her, Andrew ducked his head. "Oh." He reached into his back pocket and withdrew a surprisingly clean handkerchief. "I must look a sight." As much as possible, he cleaned the dirt and dust from his face, grimacing when he saw the now dark handkerchief. Meeting her gaze again, a twinkle lit his honey-colored eyes as he added, "Quite a difference from the last time you took note of me on board a ship."

Her cheeks warmed, though not the searing heat she'd experienced then. Oh, what an aggravating man to remind her of that.

"I believe I prefer the coal dust," she countered, daring him to deliver a retort.

Instead he quirked his eyebrows and regarded her with surprise, as if he couldn't believe she would say such a thing. "I believe you said you have a message for me?"

Yes. Back to business. A much safer subject than their lighthearted banter. That sent her thoughts in a direction she'd much rather not pursue.

After wetting her lips, Grace swallowed and forced a calm composure. "Uncle Richard asked me to come fetch you. He'd like to see you in his office at your earliest convenience."

Andrew furrowed his brow. "Did he happen to say what this is regarding?"

"No." She shook her head. "He only said he wished you to come to him."

"Very well." He held out his hands and inspected them, giving them and the state of his clothes a wary glance. "I will attempt to wash up and be there directly."

Grace opened her mouth to tell him she'd wait, but that would be completely inappropriate. It would also leave her standing there, thinking thoughts best left ignored. They would venture into dangerous territory, and she needed to keep a clear head. So instead she nodded.

"All right. I will inform him you're on your way."

"Thank you." And with that, he turned tail, disappearing from view around the far side of the ship.

She stood and stared at that spot for several minutes. Then she shook herself from the reverie and turned back toward her uncle's office. She'd just told herself she didn't need any distractions, and then she'd allowed Andrew to do just that. It'd be best if she went back to work and put the disturbing image of Andrew washing the grime from his clothes out of her head.

But about thirty minutes later, in walked the man who wouldn't leave her thoughts, looking as fresh as the morning dew, his hair wet and slicked back. He'd changed his shirt, too, though the one he now wore had several wet spots from the remaining water in his hair. Heading straight for her uncle's office, Andrew barely acknowledged her as he rapped three times on the closed door. A muffled voice from within beckoned him to enter. With a nod in her direction, he entered, closing the door behind him.

Grace wanted to move closer to the door to see if she could hear anything at all about what they discussed. But her uncle's receptionist would have something to say about that. So she went back to work and focused all her efforts on the filing.

After what seemed like just a few brief minutes, the door to her uncle's office opened, and Andrew stepped out. "Thank you very much, Mr. Baxton. I am grateful you agree." He touched two fingers to his forehead, where a stubborn lock of hair curled down across his brow. "Miss Baxton."

He left almost as quickly as he'd arrived. Grace turned her head from the front door to her uncle's office, where he stood in the doorway, watching her. A silent nod beckoned her to join him, and she did. With the door again closed, her uncle stepped behind his desk and took a seat, inviting her to do the same.

"I suppose you have a lot of questions," he began, steepling his fingers as he rested his elbows on his desk.

Of course she did. A meeting he'd made to sound extremely important and confidential, and it had only lasted mere minutes? Grace perched on the edge of her seat and opened her mouth, about to let loose with the slew of questions she had, when her uncle held up one hand.

"Before you ask, I will tell you that I have declared Andrew's sentence fulfilled in terms of repaying his debt."

"You did what?" Grace covered her mouth at the escaped words. She should bite her tongue and wait for her uncle to finish. "I am sorry, Uncle. That was quite ill-mannered of me. Please continue."

Her uncle cleared his throat. "Indeed. Now, as I said, Andrew no longer has to work for us, but he has asked to continue for the remainder of his assigned sentence." He shrugged. "Said he wanted to send money back to his family. He has been quite advantageous to the workload here at the docks, and I would be a fool had I denied his request."

Money for his family? Grace had been certain he came from a station very similar to her own. Perhaps not quite as affluent, but close. Why would he need to earn money? And why send it to his family instead of keeping it for his own needs?

"So he will remain working for you for another six weeks?" she asked, since her other questions would have to be answered by Andrew himself.

"Yes," her uncle replied. "At that time, we will revisit his employment and it will again be his choice to stay or leave."

Grace couldn't decide if she liked the idea of him staying or if she wanted him to leave. She'd already come to terms with him serving a sentence in working for them, but for him to be there of his own accord, and earning a wage as well? That changed things a great deal.

"Now, if you don't mind, Grace," her uncle continued. "I have work that requires my attention."

Her uncle's dismissal was clear. She took her leave and returned to the front room. Again sliding into the systematic groove of filing, Grace let her mind entertain several possible answers to her questions. At least with Andrew staying, she had the chance to probe deeper and find out more about him. That was one point in his favor. But would Andrew answer the questions she asked? Or would he remain as silent about his affairs as he'd been in response to her apology a few weeks ago? Only one way to find out.

Chapter 11

"Do you enjoy making repairs such as that?"

Grace sat on a bench opposite Andrew, who perched on a crate near the brigantine where he worked that day. Dressed much like he had been for most of the days she'd seen him, at least today his clothing hadn't been ruined by coal dust. He held a heavy-cabled net in his hands as he ran his fingers over the cross-knots, checking for frays and areas that needed reinforcement.

He shrugged without looking up. "It certainly beats hauling waste to the barrels or scrubbing floors."

"But you have scrubbed the decks of some of these ships during your time working at the docks."

"That's different."

"How so?" Grace had attempted to engage Andrew in conversation several times that week. Today marked the third time in as many days, yet he hadn't been any more talkative now than the other two previous days.

"It just is."

That line of questioning clearly wasn't working. "You must have spent a lot of time around the water and various ships." Perhaps appealing to his pride by noting his obvious skills would produce better results. "You know quite a lot about them, and my uncle has remarked more than once about the asset you have been to the workers here."

"I am no stranger to ships," he replied, "but my skills don't come from extensive experience with them. Working with my hands is simply something I enjoy, no matter what the task."

That sounded a lot like her uncle. He made no attempt to hide his distaste for paperwork and being isolated in a dark office.

"Is that what you did before you—" No wait. That wouldn't do. She couldn't remind him of why he ended up working for them. He'd clam up for certain. Not that he cooperated all that much now. "Before you came to work for my uncle?" she ended up asking.

"Tasks with my hands?" He actually looked up at her with that one. "Sometimes."

And back to his work. Grace sighed. This proved harder than she thought it'd be. Either her questions needed a little refining to become more appealing to Andrew, or she needed to improve her delivery.

"You have been with us for nearly seven weeks, yet you haven't requested any time to visit your family. Do they not live near enough for you to do so?"

A tic pulsed in his cheek, and his jaw moved back and forth, almost as if he was grinding his teeth or attempting to hold back a groan.

"They are aware of my whereabouts, and as you might recall, I have been serving a judicial sentence for my crimes." His words came out through clenched teeth. "Assignments like that don't usually afford the opportunity for visits home."

Perfect. She wanted to avoid reminding him of the deed that had brought him together with her family, and now she'd gone and done just that. Maybe if she focused on his exemplary work that led to Uncle Richard forgiving his debt early.

"But you are now working for wage with my uncle. He declared your debt paid in full five days ago. Does that not change anything?"

"Nothing of consequence." Andrew took a deep breath, and his expression relaxed. "It merely means I am earning a sum for what I do instead of being forced to toil at whatever task is deemed appropriate."

"And you are free to use that money however you wish." Grace wanted to ask about him sending money home, but he didn't seem all too eager to speak of his family. "That must make a substantial difference in how you view the work you do."

"I do whatever is asked of me with the same level of devotion, whether someone is paying me to do a job or not."

Uncle Richard had said as much to her the other day. And Harriet had mentioned more than once how much the rest of the staff at the manor liked Andrew. For a man who had only been with them such a short time, he had accomplished quite a lot. His actions spoke a great deal to his impeccable character, even if he could be rather vexing at times.

"Many of our staff have noticed your dedication and have spoken of it."

"They will do that," he replied without emotion.

Back to the single-phrase replies. Either he was oblivious to her attempts at gathering information from him, or he intentionally offered the least amount possible. She leaned more toward the latter.

"So you view all of your duties equally?"

"Yes."

A spark of mischief lit inside her, and she smiled. "Even when that task involves hauling waste and dumping it in barrels?"

Finally the faintest hint of a grin formed on his lips. She might wear him down yet.

"Yes, even then."

Andrew peered at Grace through half-lidded eyes. For the third time that week, she had sought him out, initially claiming to need his assistance for this or that. It didn't take long though before she launched into her barrage of questions about his past. He did his best to respond without being impolite, but no matter what he said, she had another question to immediately follow.

"And what about mucking out stalls or polishing saddles with Jesse there to provoke you?"

He raised his head to look across the way at her. If he didn't know better, he'd swear she was baiting him. She wouldn't do that, would she? Then again, if her amusing attempts to coax information from him had failed, humor might prove more successful. He'd better watch himself or she might actually find a way to break down his carefully constructed barriers.

"Jesse is nothing more than a self-appointed peacock with more fluff to his tail feathers than substance." Andrew rolled his eyes. "His actions are of no concern to me."

"I must say, he isn't the same now that you're no longer there for him to antagonize. Poor Willie is back to bearing the brunt of the torment."

"If Willie is anything like I saw, he can handle himself with Jesse." And more, if Andrew didn't miss his guess. That young lad had quite a bit of spunk in him. "I'd be more concerned for Jesse than Willie."

"You do have a point."

The sound of her melodious laughter worked its way into his defenses more than he cared to admit. The way she sat on that bench, her ankles neatly tucked beneath her with her hands primly folded in her lap, made it seem as if she waited for a friend. No one would suspect she had ulterior motives.

"And you seem to know quite a lot about Jesse's type," Grace continued.

"We have a pair of stable hands much like him and Willie."

Her entire face lit up at that remark. Oh no. She'd done it. She'd managed to get him to let down his guard for just one second, and now he'd admitted to having a stable as well as servants to work there. He didn't want to keep everything about his past from her. He just didn't want anyone feeling sorry for him. So he said the least he could. Unfortunately staying quiet proved more and more difficult with Miss Baxton around.

"Oh? Do you ride? Or is that for someone else in your family? Perhaps a brother or sister?"

"I go out every once in a while," he replied.

No way would she trick him again. He'd pay much closer attention. Of course, that might have been what got him into trouble in the first place. Watching her too closely only distracted him.

And that dress. He couldn't remember a more suitable shade of blue. The same color as her often mesmerizing eyes. With at least a dozen buttons on the front of the jacket and lace trim at the neck and sleeves as well as across the middle of her skirt, Grace presented the picture of perfect femininity. Even her bonnet matched, right down to the lace ties. Charming and attractive both came to mind. And that was a very dangerous combination.

"Bradenton!"

James Woodruff's voice called out from the deck of the brigantine. Andrew looked up.

"You finished with that net yet?" Woodruff glanced from him to Grace and back again.

Andrew glanced at the item tangled in his fingers. He'd actually been finished with it for a little while now, but he'd tarried to remain with Grace. "Yes, it's done."

"Good. Come back on board. I've got another task in mind for you." Another look at Grace, and he disappeared over the starboard side.

Andrew gathered up the net in his arms and stood. Grace did the same.

"Miss Baxton, do forgive me this abrupt departure, but it appears I am needed on the ship."

Grace twisted the tip of her parasol against the ground. "No apologies necessary, Mr. Bradenton. I have taken up more than enough of your time already."

As much as he would rather sit with her, he did have a job to do. But Andrew didn't want to leave in such a brusque manner. He grinned.

"Perhaps our next conversation will result in a more successful outcome to your inquisition attempts."

She lowered her lashes and a pretty shade of pink filled her cheeks. He didn't exactly leave her with much to say in response. So he changed the subject.

"Will I see you at the festival on Saturday?"

Surprise filled her face at that. "Yes. I'll be there with my family."

Touching two fingers to the brim of his cap, he winked. "Until then, Miss Baxton."

Walking away from her proved harder than he'd thought. He wanted to turn around, to see if she watched his departure. But that might make him change his mind. He took a deep breath and forced himself to stay focused. Just like his reasons for asking Mr. Baxton to stay on in spite of being given his freedom. Grace had factored rather heavily into them. He wasn't ready to say good-bye to her just yet. But he'd never admit it to anyone.

"Uncle Richard!" Grace sat up straight and pressed her arm against the side cushion of their open carriage. "I see Maureen over by the ticket booth. May I please join her?"

They had just arrived on the edge of the park a few streets north of the shipyards. What a sight to behold! There had to be hundreds of people gathered on the grassy area, and that didn't include the number in small dinghies or rowboats on the river, or even those enjoying a swim in the chilly water. It might be July, but she'd stepped in that river on the hottest day of the year, and even then she couldn't last long.

Her aunt and uncle exchanged a silent glance between them, their unspoken communication saying more than any words might say. Grace prayed they'd agree.

"Yes," Aunt Charlotte answered for him. "But mind your manners and stay away from the deeper throes of the masses."

Uncle Richard signaled to Matthew to stop the carriage long enough for Grace to accept his assistance and climb down. She released his hand and offered a reassuring smile to them both. But it was Aunt Charlotte's expression that caught her eye. She grinned and winked. Grace returned the wink and fairly skipped to join her friend. Her aunt was a true kindred spirit.

"Maureen!" Grace waved her handkerchief in the air.

Her friend looked from left to right and smiled when she saw Grace. The two clasped hands and exchanged a quick kiss on the cheek.

"I was hoping you would be here today." Maureen placed her gloved hand over her mouth to conceal a yawn. "It's been a day full of events, but I am not fond of the crowd. I even left my maid on the blanket with my family over there." She gestured a few yards away, then turned an earnest gaze on Grace. "You will stay with me, right?"

"Of course." Grace nodded and drew her friend into a hug. "When I saw you, I begged my aunt and uncle to let me leave the carriage." She placed a hand across her brow and feigned the act of fainting. "I would simply swoon from the trials of enduring several hours standing amidst my family with no one my own age to share the fun."

Maureen pressed a gloved hand to her lips and laughed. "Oh, Grace, I am happy you're here to make this day much better."

Grace tucked Maureen's arm into the crook of her own. "Come then. Let us not tarry another moment." She led them closer to the center of the festivities so they could better hear what was taking place.

"Hooray!" The crowd responded in hearty agreement, the cheers drowning out the speaker's next words.

Grace stood on tiptoe to see over the heads, trying to identify the man in the middle of the group. Why could they not have chosen a spot a bit higher on a hill? If only the woman holding the parasol over her head would step a little to the left, Grace could see.

"There has to be another way."

She huffed and took a few steps toward a bench and scrambled to her task before Maureen could stop her.

"Grace!" Maureen gasped. "Someone will see you there."

"But I cannot abide not seeing who is speaking. Everyone is all in a twitter. I simply must find out."

"Well, don't include me in this scheme. I remain innocent if someone from your family or mine discovers you."

Grace grinned at Maureen's folded arms as her friend turned her back. She wasn't deterred by the antics though and focused once more on her goal.

"At last!"

Maureen's reaction belied her uninterest as she unfolded her arms and pressed against Grace, straining on tiptoe. "What is it you see?"

Grace swayed to the left and right. "Oh, it's Mayor Rhoads." She craned her neck and stretched her ear closer to the sounds booming from the central stage. She rapidly patted Maureen on the shoulder. "He just announced the arrival of electric streetcars and said they will slowly begin to replace the horse-drawn cars in Wilmington."

"Really?"

"Yes, something about the United States having forty-three states now, with Idaho just being added, and how we need to progress if we are to keep the pace with the other states."

"My father mentioned the other day that Wyoming is due to be added to the union any day now as well."

Grace looked down at her friend. "All right. Forty-four states then."

Amazing to consider how fast the country grew with each passing day. Every time she turned around, there seemed to be something new and exciting taking place.

From lightbulbs, to telephones, to talking machines, and now electric street cars.

"What is happening now?"

Her friend's voice broke into her thoughts and brought her back to the present. Grace once again pushed up on her feet, only this time, she lost her balance.

Panic struck her as she flailed her arms in an attempt to stand. She only caught a glimpse of the terror on Maureen's face before an arm snaked around her waist and held her upright. Her breath escaped in one swoosh, while her heart pounded in her chest.

"Mercy!" Grace placed one hand on her chest and turned to see who had rescued her. "I do apologize for my clumsiness, but—"

"I commend you, Miss Baxton, on your ingenious method of observing the proceedings at the park center," Andrew began with a twinkle in his warm eyes. "But I daresay there is another, safer, place where you might still be able to see."

Maureen giggled from her place beside Andrew. Were it not for the commanding way his gaze held hers, Grace would have leveled a glare at her friend for not warning her. Instead she couldn't look away.

Finally finding her voice, she parried his teasing with "You are no doubt correct, Mr. Bradenton, but I find the view from this position to be quite to my liking."

A smile tugged at his lips. "Then perhaps you should make certain you are tied to the bench in order to preserve your balance."

"And risk appearing even more foolish?"

Maureen shamelessly stood there with open amusement on her face. Mindful of their unexpected companion, Grace only silently scolded her friend, making a vow to speak with her later. She accepted Andrew's assistance and returned again to the ground.

Andrew nodded toward the crowd, where voices continued to be raised and declarations were issued from the middle of the throngs. "I gather you are in favor of these new streetcars for the city?"

"Of course!" Grace replied. "Why would I not?"

"No reason. I am merely surprised to see you so interested in developments such as this."

Grace tried not to take offense at his words. He likely didn't intend them to be an insult in any way. She might often be more interested in the people and the social aspects of the city, but Aunt Charlotte remained quite involved and informed, and she made sure Grace and her children did, too.

"As you know, I do read a lot." He should know that from his remarks about how often he caught her with books when he worked at their manor. "And I pay attention when pivotal changes are in the offing."

"Ah, so you stay abreast of the political developments taking place in this area?"

"Not as much as the social changes, but I am aware of most of them."

Andrew glanced toward the center of the crowd, his height affording him a view Grace envied. As much as she longed to again see what was happening, she didn't dare attempt to use the bench a second time. Besides, Maureen might faint away from the shock of it all. At the moment, she remained a silent observer, while providing Grace with a necessary chaperone.

"Well, do allow me to join you ladies then, and we shall enjoy the festivities as well as the forthcoming fireworks on the river."

Grace shot a silent look to her friend, and Maureen

nodded. She turned back to Andrew. "I could think of nothing I would like more, Mr. Bradenton."

As he moved to stand behind them both, Grace looked at Maureen from the corner of her eye. She couldn't say anything now, but her friend would no doubt discuss this meeting in great detail once they were alone.

Chapter 12

Feeling like a waiter with the four dishes he balanced, Andrew lowered himself to his knees with great care onto the blanket beside Grace. She jumped in response. Almost as if she didn't expect him to join her.

"Sorry. I didn't mean to scare you."

He held out a dish with vanilla ice cream in it and fumbled with two tin cups of water while settling his own dish in his lap.

She took the dish in one hand and waved off his comment with the other before accepting the tin cup as well. "It's all right. I must have been daydreaming." Grace avoided his eyes and instead paid close attention to her dessert.

Her voice trembled a little. She wasn't comfortable. That much was clear. But what had happened from the time they left her family to now? He assessed the spot she'd chosen before he'd gone in search of their sweet treat. Blankets of every pattern and color spread out like a patchwork quilt all across the grassy park. A handful of people weaved their way between those seated, but most of those gathered had found a place to relax while waiting for the explosive show.

Maureen sat with Grace's Aunt Anastasia on another blanket just a few feet away, but the rest of her family had found a spot somewhere else in the park. Now Andrew wondered if he'd been wrong to suggest they share a spot. She didn't need to see his hesitation though. Grace was already nervous.

"See? What did I tell you?" Andrew announced with forced pride. "This is the perfect spot."

Grace looked around them with a guarded expression. "It is a bit closer to the water than I expected. That's for certain." She hesitated a moment then nodded. "But it does appear to be a good choice. We will have an excellent view of the fireworks."

Andrew snapped his fingers and pointed at her. "Exactly."

She took a spoonful of ice cream but still looked to the left and right, as if trying to determine if anyone was watching them. He was the one who had to be on his best behavior. Having Grace's aunt and friend sitting so close, they would see every move he made for certain. With that in mind, she had nothing to worry about. So why was she so jumpy?

"Did you have to go far to get these?"

Andrew jerked his gaze back to hers and stuttered. "Oh, um, not at all." At least it didn't seem that far to him. Then again, Grace had become quite nervous from the time he'd left her to the time he'd returned. So maybe it had been farther than he'd thought.

Grace shifted her focus and regarded her dessert as if

it held some special secret. "This is quite delicious. One of the best dishes I've had in quite some time."

Her voice was so soft he had to strain to hear her above the lapping of the water against the riverbanks and the noise from the crowd.

"Have you enjoyed the festival so far?"

Grace looked at him and smiled, her entire face lighting up, despite only having the torches to illuminate the park. "Immensely! It is an ideal culmination to the week."

"Well, I have to work tomorrow," he pointed out, "but the next day we have Sunday services. That's a good end…or start…to the week, depending on how you look at it."

"I agree." She took a sip of water and lowered her cup. "And what are your thoughts about tonight?"

He winked. "I believe the company I've kept this evening has made it more pleasant than had I remained where I was."

She glanced over his shoulder to where her friend and aunt sat. "Yes, even if we must endure the close inspection of watchful eyes." Grace nodded her head in their direction. "I can only imagine what they might be saying."

"Oh, you can be certain they are talking about us… or at least me, at any rate." He set down his cup and dish and placed his right hand flat across his chest. "But I vow to be absolutely above reproach this entire time. You won't even find a speck of dirt on my clothing." He glanced down and pretended to flick off a speck or two.

Grace giggled. "You'd better, or I'll be the one who will not hear the end of it."

Good. He'd managed to get her laughing again. And she didn't seem as nervous as when he'd first joined her. Now to keep her relaxed.

"Do you mean to say your friend wouldn't give you

the benefit of the doubt where I'm concerned?" He dished up a heaping spoonful of ice cream and stuck it into his mouth.

"Not at all," she immediately countered. "In fact, Maureen would be the first to become the leader of the inquisition, followed closely behind by my Aunt 'Stasia."

After swallowing, Andrew pressed his tongue against one side of his teeth and nodded. "I believe I'm beginning to understand why your uncle agreed so readily to us not joining them. They have a built-in scout network to report back to them on every detail."

Grace slid her spoon slowly from her mouth and swallowed her ice cream. Andrew had to force himself not to focus on her lips.

"More so than that," she replied. "I believe Maureen is merely looking out for her own interests and building up material she can use against me should I catch her in a similar situation. Rumor has it there is a certain young gentleman who has been escorting her home from my aunt's bookshop." Grace smiled and took a drink from her tin cup.

Andrew waggled his eyebrows. "Ah-ha. That explains it. She's besotted."

Her lips tightened, preventing the water she'd just drunk from escaping.

He laughed and took a drink as he attempted to school his expression into one of nonchalance. It was no use. "I'm sorry," he said through barely contained chuckles. "I do thank you though, for sparing me the spray of your drink."

With a swallow and dainty clearing of her throat, Grace regained her composure. "You are most welcome," she replied, raising her cup again to her lips. "But I cannot guarantee that should a repeat occurrence take place, you will remain free from harm."

It took Andrew a moment to process what she'd just said. He narrowed his eyes at the playful, underlying threat laced between her words. She spoke with such calm, her expression devoid of any mischief. He couldn't tell if she was flirting or serious. And she likely preferred it that way. Such a unique blend of sophistication and affability.

He finished his dessert and took a sip of his own water, then turned toward a makeshift stage not too far away where a band had assembled. Almost instantly, the rousing strains of celebratory music filled the cool night air. "What do you think?"

"About your sense of humor or the music currently playing and the ambience of the festival?" She took a final spoonful of her ice cream, the corners of her lips turning up slightly as she savored the last remnants.

"My—" He paused. Wait a minute. Had she just given him a taste of his own medicine? He clenched his jaw and raised his chin a fraction of an inch. "The festival, of course."

She swallowed and washed down her dessert with another drink. "In that case, I approve. The city has truly outdone itself with the vendors, the performances on some of the other stages, the entertainment, and soon the fireworks."

He leaned back on his left elbow and regarded her through half-lidded eyes. "And here I thought the ice cream would be the climax of the evening."

Grace covered her mouth and giggled. "I am sorry, Mr. Bradenton, but even such delectable ice cream pales in comparison to fireworks and lively music."

Andrew held up his cup with his right hand and tipped

it in her direction. "I am not so certain. I have had some flavors that seemed to dance in my mouth with their stimulating tastes."

After taking another sip of water, she lowered the cup and looked at him over the rim with a grin. "Ah, it seems you have an overdeveloped sweet tooth, Mr. Bradenton. First it was the candied apples. Then the sugar sticks. And finally the ice cream. It's a wonder you still have all your teeth."

He tipped his cup toward her. "I'll have you know our cook prepares delicious meals three times a day and makes sure each one of us eats some of everything she's made."

Grace paused with her cup midway to her mouth and stared, her lips parted. "So you *do* have a cook! I knew it."

Oh no! She'd done it again. Caused him to let down his guard and share more about his past. How did she manage it so easily?

"Yes, I admit it. My family employs a cook." He might as well give in this time. She'd been relentless about divining information from him, and in such a charming manner, too. So far he'd received nothing remotely close to pity for what he'd temporarily given up, so why had he been so worried about that?

She cocked her head and remained silent for several moments. Andrew could feel the heat warm his neck and creep toward his cheeks. If she started to believe he'd answer anything, there'd be no end to the long line of questions she'd ask.

"I can understand that," she finally said with a nod. "Nearly all of the families in this area have a cook to prepare their meals."

Andrew pressed his lips into a thin line. Now was the

time to truly come clean. They'd enjoyed quite a bit of banter, and he couldn't remember the last time he'd been so relaxed in the company of a lady. If he continued to clam up, he'd lose everything he'd gained where Grace was concerned.

"This is true. Employing a cook is not uncommon. But my mother isn't as involved as most ladies of their homes." He tilted his head and stared up at the stars in the night sky. "She's had to endure several surgeries of late, and I'm afraid they've taken their toll on her strength. The doctors didn't know what was wrong. She's been confined to a bed for months now."

Grace yanked a stem of a dandelion weed from the ground and twirled it between her fingers. "You mentioned the surgeries the day we first met. How the doctors' bills had driven you to such extreme measures."

Andrew pushed himself to a sitting position and set aside his cup. Softening his voice, he added, "Yes, then I heard one doctor tell my father it was likely a tumor that could be cancer, and I prayed to God it wasn't true. When the doctor spoke of an operation that could potentially save her life, I formed that foolhardy plan." He sighed and mumbled as he reached for a blade of grass and twisted it back and forth. "But you couldn't possibly understand."

A pained expression flitted across her face before she had the chance to hide it. "Actually, you might be surprised. Our worlds and experiences might be more similar than you'd imagine."

Now Andrew hadn't expected that. Pity? Yes. Blame? Perhaps. Derision? Most certainly. But empathy? Not in the least. And she looked like she had a story to tell. Perhaps it would help him feel less like a man on an island in all of this. He took her dish and cup from her and set them on his other side; then he reached out and covered the hand in her lap with his own. "Tell me about it…please?"

Grace looked down at the hand covering hers, his tanned skin a stark contrast to her pale tone. She glanced behind him toward Maureen and Aunt 'Stasia. They seemed rather engrossed in their own conversation, so she returned her attention to Andrew and gave him a wary look.

"Are you certain you wish to know? It might affect the preconceived notions you've formed about my family and me."

Andrew stiffened, and Grace immediately regretted how harsh her words had sounded. But she had grown tired of his assumptions and generalizations without knowing the truth. He sighed and nodded.

"Yes, I do. I would not have asked otherwise."

She looked across the river and took a deep breath. It had been eight years, but in some ways, it felt like yesterday.

"Well, you already know I live with my aunt and uncle."

He nodded, giving her hand a squeeze. "Yes, and your uncle told me it was because of an accident that took the lives of your parents."

Moisture formed at the corners of her eyes, but she blinked it away. "An accident that also left me without the use of my legs. I was in a wheeled chair for several months."

His eyes widened at that, but he didn't say a word. So she continued.

"I, too, endured endless visits with specialists and doctors following the accident. And it came down to a single operation that could give me back the use of my legs or cripple me permanently." She sighed. "My uncle was already dealing with financial struggles, and the transfer of the assets from the shipping company was delayed. The added expense of my visits only made the situation worse." Grace stared out in the general direction of where her family sat. "I must admit, seeing my young cousins with my aunt and uncle just a bit ago started me thinking. They have given up so much for me. Sometimes it makes me feel guilty for the burden I was at the time." She mumbled under her breath. "And in some ways still am."

He snapped his fingers. "I knew something had happened."

She shook her head and turned to face him. "What do you mean?"

Andrew pulled back and rested his forearms on his knees. Grace immediately felt the loss of warmth from his withdrawn hand, but his nearness still offered a great deal of comfort in its place.

"I noticed when I first sat down here tonight that you seemed a bit distracted. And you weren't yourself. That easygoing manner of yours was missing."

Grace ducked her chin. "Oh." And she had hoped her teasing remarks and smiles might cover up her pensive thoughts. Obviously it hadn't. Andrew had seen right through her unsuccessful attempts.

She saw his hand before his fingers touched her chin as he raised her head to meet his gaze. "Hey," he said softly, "I am every bit as guilty of lumping far too much weight on my own shoulders. It would be wrong of me to blame you for doing the same."

He moved his index finger back and forth on the underside of her chin. She quelled the shiver that started somewhere near the base of her spine. Instead she got lost in the caramel-colored depths of his caring eyes.

As if he had read her mind, he jerked his hand back and put some distance between them.

"Sorry about that." He averted his gaze for a brief second then released a short sigh. "It's clear the operation was a success." He gestured toward her legs. "I mean, you are obviously walking, and I don't recall noticing a limp of any kind."

Grace blinked a few times. The operation? Oh, right. She'd better get a handle on her emotions. And fast.

"Yes, thanks to my aunt and a bazaar she'd organized, we received a generous donation that allowed us to make an appointment with one of the best surgeons in his field."

A dimple in his right cheek appeared, accompanying his grin. "Well, I am grateful it was a success. Otherwise I'd have had to brush up on my skills at pushing a wheeled chair through the grass." He wiggled his eyebrows. "And you would be decidedly taller than me sitting on this blanket."

Grace smiled at his antics. How good it felt to laugh and share a common bond. They had definitely reached a new level in their relationship, whatever it was at the moment. She started to respond when his face turned serious again.

"Thank you, Miss Baxton, for sharing what you did. And I apologize for my wrong assumptions where you're concerned. I'll try not to make the same mistake again."

"You're quite welcome, Mr. Bradenton." She nearly stumbled over his formal name. In all her thoughts, she called him Andrew. It grew increasingly harder to remind herself not to call him such verbally.

As if he'd read her mind, he cleared his throat. "Yes,

about that." He once again held her gaze. "Might I have your permission to call you by your given name? After tonight, addressing you as 'Miss Baxton' does not feel right anymore." He held up his index finger. "But only if you will also agree to call me Andrew."

Relieved he'd been the one to suggest it, Grace nodded. "Yes, you may. And I agree."

"Excellent. Glad that's settled." Andrew looked toward the river then back at her. "Now, it looks like the fireworks are about to start." He lowered his left arm and silently invited her to move closer. "Are you ready?"

She didn't know if he referred to the Independence Day celebration or where their relationship was headed. Or both. Either way, she could answer in the affirmative. With a glance behind his back at Maureen and Aunt 'Stasia, who both grinned and nodded their encouragement, Grace shifted closer to Andrew and allowed him to rest his arm around her back.

As the night sky lit up with a blaze of flashing color and exploding fire, a nagging reminder flitted through her head. At least she could show her appreciation for the enjoyable evening they'd shared.

"In case I forget to tell you later," she said without looking at him, "thank you for joining me tonight. And for listening."

He turned his head toward her, making her acutely aware of how close they sat. "You're quite welcome," he said. "We should do it again."

"Perhaps." She grinned. "Next year around this time."

She felt rather than saw his surprise in the way his arm flexed against her back, and Grace realized what she'd just said. One year from now? She didn't even know if he'd be there five *weeks* from now, let alone a full year.

But just as she was about to retract what she'd said, he jumped in with a reply.

"You can count on it."

Chapter 13

Andrew stepped outside the Wise & Weldon Lumberyard and looked up and down the street. He didn't get to that area of Market Street often. Since the proprietor informed him it would take about an hour to collect the order Mr. Baxton had placed three weeks ago, he had plenty of time to do a little detective work.

It had been three days since Grace shared about her own surgery and all her aunt had done to help. Not only had he misjudged Grace and her family, but his thievery had cost them precious items. Mr. Baxton might have declared his debt paid through the work he'd done, but what they'd lost couldn't be replaced with mere money or time served. He had to do something.

Glancing around the various business establishments on both sides of the street, Andrew's eyes alighted on a sign positioned on the third floor of a brick building just a few hundred feet away, C. F. Thomas and Company.

The ample display of books and stationery in the storefront windows gave him an idea.

"Perfect!" he said out loud to himself.

After he looked up and down the street, Andrew crossed to the other side, whistling as he walked. This should get him started in the right direction.

The bell above the door jingled as he entered, and he stepped into the musty yet clean shop. In the far corner, an impressive printing press stood like a sentinel announcing its prominent function. He looked straight back where a man wearing an apron soiled with ink stood in front of another machine Andrew didn't recognize.

"I shall be with you momentarily," the man called out, peering to the front of the shop through the parts of the machine he operated.

"I'm in no rush," Andrew called back.

He stepped closer to a rack advertising used books. Quite a collection the proprietor had amassed. And their condition nearly rivaled that of the brand-new books on the next rack. If only he could remember the name of the ones he'd taken from the Baxton manor. But even reading the ones on the shelf didn't jog his memory.

"My apologies, sir," the man with the apron said as he approached the counter. "But my assistant is not in today, and I fear I am forced to do the work of two people." He wiped his hands on his apron. "Charles Thomas, at your service. How may I assist you?"

"Andrew Bradenton," Andrew replied. "I work for Hannsen & Baxton Shipping."

"Ah yes." Thomas nodded. "A notable and well-respected company."

"From what I've heard and seen, yes." He gestured around the expansive storeroom. "You have quite an impressive establishment here as well."

Mr. Thomas raised his chin an inch or two and stuck out his chest. "Yes, we recently expanded to double our previous space. It has been excellent for business." He raised his eyebrows then puffed out his cheeks as he blew out air. "But it has meant an increased demand in the personnel required to keep the shop running."

"I can well imagine that." Andrew pointed toward the machine in the back. "What is that you were working on a moment ago?"

Thomas's eyes lit up and he returned to the machine, setting his hand on top like he would a son or even a valued employee. "This? This is the J. L. Morrison Cast-Iron Book Binding Machine, straight from New York." His hand slid across the top almost in a caress. "One of our recent acquisitions for the expansion, and my pride and joy."

Andrew smiled. "That I can see."

The man cleared his throat. "Yes, well, the patented spring-feed gear gives automatic adjustment to any size wire for the wire stitching. It will greatly improve my output for our pamphlets and blank books, another part of our increased development." Thomas moved back behind the counter and regarded Andrew with a quizzical eye. "Now, enough about me. What is it that brought you here this fine morning, and how may I be of assistance?"

Ah yes. Business. It would be so easy to peruse the various product outputs in the shop, connecting the merchandise with the paper milled at one of his father's mills. Quite the experience seeing things from this end of the manufacturing line. But his hour of free time was disappearing with each passing minute.

"To be honest," Andrew began, "I am not certain where to start."

"Usually at the beginning," Thomas said with a grin.

Andrew chuckled. The man was likable. No doubt about it. "Yes. But I'm afraid that will take too long to tell. Suffice it to say, I am in search of some rare and valuable books that were recently lost to a family in Brandywine."

"What are the titles?"

"Unfortunately I don't know them offhand." Andrew sighed. "I hadn't intended to come here today, but I had some additional time come available to me, so I decided it might be worthwhile." He held up his index finger. "I can get the titles from a member of the family though."

Thomas rubbed his thumb and forefinger across his smooth chin then adjusted the wire-rimmed spectacles resting on his nose. "Hmm. I cannot say for certain, but my best advice would be to inquire with Joseph and William Adams. They operate Adams & Brother General Variety Store, and they have four stories of commodities of all shapes and sizes. If there have been any valuable books circulating at any point throughout this city or area, they would know about it."

"Splendid!" Andrew stretched his arm across the counter. "Thank you. This has helped a great deal."

Thomas accepted the handshake. "My pleasure, young man. If I can be of any further assistance, if you have any print or binding needs, do come back and see me again."

Andrew touched the brim of his cap. "I will do that. Good day to you, sir."

"And a good day to you," the man replied.

With a spring in his step, Andrew headed outside to the sidewalk once more. He withdrew his pocket watch and flipped it open. Thirty-five minutes left. Just enough time to stop by the bank. After patting his back pocket and feeling the slight bump from the bills he'd placed there, he turned to the left and walked the two blocks north.

He paused outside the ornate SaVille Building at the corner of Sixth and Market Streets and closed his eyes. He opened them again and glanced across the street to SaVille Wines & Liquors. A part of him was tempted to go there and pay a visit to Alexander SaVille. See what new stock he had. At one time, it would have been quite easy, but not anymore. After inhaling and exhaling two deep breaths, Andrew placed his hand on the door to the bank and pushed it open, praying this visit would go well.

"Well, well, well," a jeering voice greeted him. "If it isn't the prodigal son of the mill owner, finally deciding to grace our bank with his presence again."

Andrew forced a grin to his lips and turned to face Henry Johnston, one of the proprietors of the bank. If he didn't keep his voice down, Alfred Elliott would come out to greet him as well.

"So, Mr. Bradenton has decided to return."

Too late.

The other proprietor stepped out of his office and leaned against the doorframe, folding his arms across his chest. "To what do we owe this pleasure?"

He should have known he wouldn't be able to set foot inside this building without Al and Henry seeing him. They'd been friends for a good many years. His absence of late wouldn't change that. Andrew nodded to each man in turn.

"Good morning, Henry, Al."

"Why so formal and distant, Drew?" Henry asked. Stepping forward, he added, "It's good to see you again." He pulled him into a quick hug, giving Andrew's back three firm thumps before backing away.

"Yes," Andrew replied. "And I'm sorry I haven't been

here in a while." He glanced around the open area of the bank's lobby. "I can't stay long, but some things have happened that have kept me away."

Henry gestured for Al to join them and extended his arm toward his private office. It looked the same as it always did. Papers stacked in several piles on his desk and ledgers open on every available surface. A stark contrast to Al's office, which made everyone wonder if anyone actually worked in there. Neat and tidy, with every shelf along the one wall alphabetized in exact precision. The two made a dynamic team though.

Once all three of them had taken a seat in the leather chairs in front of Henry's desk, Al was the first to speak.

"Everything *is* all right, isn't it?" He leaned forward and rested his forearms on his thighs, concern evident in his eyes. "I mean, the weekly deposits for your father's mill have still been made on schedule, but it's been done by some man named Billingsly."

"And he's been rather tight-lipped about the goings-on with you or the mill," Henry added. "I haven't been able to get a thing out of him." He smirked and leaned back in his chair, once again crossing his arms. "And believe me, I've tried."

So predictable. Andrew likely could have anticipated the entire conversation before it even happened. Henry, with his comical outlook on life, and Al, with his levelheaded approach. Andrew fell somewhere in between.

"All right," Henry continued. "Let's have it." He narrowed his eyes. "You haven't met a fair maiden, have you? Because if you have, we want to know all about it."

Andrew's thoughts immediately went to Grace. No. He'd best not go there yet. There'd be plenty of time for that later. Better stick to business for now.

"Well, you know about my mother's health," Andrew

began. Both men nodded. "And the rising bills from the doctors." He closed his eyes. *Just say it and get it over with*, he told himself. After taking a deep breath, he plunged right in. "I made a rather foolish mistake that put me in front of a judge who sentenced me to three months working for the family I'd wronged."

Henry opened his mouth to respond, but Al stayed his response with a hand. "We'd heard something along those lines but didn't want to believe it," Al said, his eyes reflecting a sincere sympathy.

"So, how did you make it here today?" Henry wanted to know. "If I count right, it's only been eight weeks."

"Well, Mr. Baxton forgave my debt a little over a week ago," Andrew replied, "but I asked to stay on and work so I could give my father the money I'd earn."

"You're working at Hannsen & Baxton?" Henry whistled long and low. "That's an impressive operation they've got going down there. You're lucky the judge didn't issue a harsher penalty."

"You don't have to tell me twice." Andrew sighed. He didn't want to dwell on the past. He reached into his back pocket to retrieve the thin stack of folded bills. "It won't undo what I did, but it will at least help a little."

Al gestured with his head toward the money. "Is that what you'd like to deposit into your father's account?"

Andrew held out the small amount. "Yes. And if you could see that Billingsly receives a note upon his next visit stating the deposit, I'd appreciate it."

"Of course." Al reached into his breast pocket and withdrew a tablet and flipped it open. After grabbing a pencil from Henry's desk, he took the money from Andrew, counted it, and made a notation in the tablet. He tucked the money into his vest pocket and returned the tablet to his coat. He set the pencil back on the desk then leveled a direct gaze at Andrew. "Is that the only reason you came in today?"

Andrew nodded and looked back and forth between the two. "That, and because I knew it was time I came by to explain what had happened." His shoulders drooped. "I really am sorry for not coming in sooner or even scribbling out a quick note to you both."

"Ah, think nothing of it," Henry replied with a wave of his hand. "We all make mistakes. And if you'd been in bigger trouble, we would have known about it." A somber expression crossed his face, so opposite of his normal affable self. "We're just glad everything is all right." He glanced at his partner and clapped him on the back. "Aren't we, Al?"

Al jerked forward from the thump and cleared his throat. "Yes. Yes, we are." He stood, and the other two followed. "Now, I am certain you have other tasks to attend to this morning. We don't wish to keep you or make you late returning." He led the way out of Henry's office and paused just outside the door, extending his hand. "Come back and see us anytime. I mean it."

Andrew shook his friend's hand. "Thank you." A moment later, the expected clap on his back came from Henry.

"Next time you can tell us all about Baxton's lovely niece." Henry leaned in between the two of them with a knowing grin and winked. "I hear she comes to the shipyard a few days every week to work for her uncle. We want to hear more about her."

Regarding them both, and seeing the undisguised interest on Henry's face coupled with the single raised eyebrow on Al's, Andrew grinned. "We shall see."

And with that, Andrew turned heel and left. A chuckle rumbled from his stomach and made his shoulders shake as he ventured outside once more. That meeting had gone better than he'd thought it would. But he shouldn't be surprised. Andrew inhaled an invigorating and cleansing breath. Just one more stop before returning to the lumberyard and then back to the docks.

"Uncle Richard?" Grace stood in the doorway to her uncle's front office, clutch and parasol in hand. "I am about to take a carriage up to Market Street to drop off Aunt Charlotte's necklace for repair. Is there anything you need while I'm out?"

Her uncle quirked his mouth and looked up before returning his eyes to her. "Umm, would you mind stopping by Diamond State Insurance for me?" He searched on his desk for something then produced a handwritten note from under one stack. "They have some rather sensitive documents for me, and I won't be able to leave here today to retrieve them."

She stepped forward to take the slip of paper from him. "Of course." Grace glanced down at the paper. "Shall I return them here or would you like them taken home where you can have them in your study there?"

"Here, please," he said without hesitation. "I have a meeting tomorrow to discuss them."

"Very well." Grace didn't question further. The partners and investors usually met monthly. Relieved she didn't have to take part in any of that, she signaled to Harriet to accompany her and left the office.

As soon as she reached the carriage Matthew had waiting, her name sounded from somewhere behind her.

"Grace!"

She turned around to see Andrew jogging toward her from the docks. "Matthew, I shall just be a minute,"

Grace called up to the driver then turned to her maid. "Harriet, you may go ahead and step inside the carriage."

After Matthew hopped down to assist Harriet, Grace walked toward Andrew and met him about halfway. "Andrew? Is there something you needed?"

He paused and bent to regain his breath, despite it being only minimally labored. "Yes," he replied once he stood straight again. "I see you're about to depart somewhere?"

Grace glanced back over her shoulder at the carriage. "I am. I have some business on Market Street for my aunt and uncle."

"Might I accompany you?"

She thought about the errand for her uncle. She could always request a binder in which she could transport the papers.

"I only ask," Andrew rushed to add, likely seeing her hesitation, "because there is one place I would like to go, and I would like you to join me."

Now that she didn't expect. He wanted her to come with him somewhere? She pressed one side of her lips together and narrowed her eyes as she regarded him. His expression didn't give away any hint of what he had in mind. Just what was he up to?

"Very well." Grace didn't know if she should trust him or not. His actions had become quite irregular all of a sudden. "I am certain Matthew will not mind taking an extra passenger. And there is more than enough room for the three of us inside."

Andrew glanced up the walkway, his brows drawn together. "The three of us?" Then he looked back at her. "Is someone else going?"

"My maid, Harriet," Grace replied. "It wouldn't be proper for me to travel alone unchaperoned." A spark of mischief lit inside. She grinned and spun on her heels. "Especially with you," she added, not giving him a chance to respond as she made her way back to the carriage.

A few seconds later, his rapid footfalls sounded behind her as he rushed to catch up with her. Placing a hand at the small of her back, he didn't say a word. She peeked at him from the corner of her eye and saw the grin tugging at his lips. At least the afternoon showed the promise of being enjoyable, and perhaps a bit entertaining.

Chapter 14

"So, what is our next destination?"

With one hand Andrew held open the door for Grace and assisted her into the carriage with his other. Harriet remained just where they'd left her, the same as with the other three stops they'd made. Sometimes he wondered about the purpose of a lady's maid, especially when they spent so much time merely accompanying their lady.

"Actually I'm done with everything I had to do this afternoon." Grace patted the satchel between her and Harriet and drew it closer to her then gave him a sly smile. "That only leaves the mysterious place you mentioned earlier."

Andrew pulled the door closed and took his seat opposite the two ladies then thumped on the roof of the carriage. A second later, Matthew slapped the reins as he called to the horses, and the carriage lurched forward.

"Mysterious?" Andrew asked once they were moving. "There isn't anything mysterious about where I'd like to go."

"Well, you were being rather vague earlier when you mentioned it." She brushed her knuckles against each other as she fiddled with them in her lap. "And I could not determine anything from your expression."

Ah, so her curiosity *had* been piqued. Andrew grinned. "That's only because I wanted it to be a surprise."

"Well Matthew might appreciate knowing where we're going, even if you insist on not telling me."

Andrew almost laughed at the affronted set of her chin and shoulders. Grace might pretend not to be interested, but by asking him to convey their destination to Matthew, she clearly hoped to gain her information that way. He pressed his lips together to suppress a chuckle and leaned back against the seat cushion.

"Matthew already knows. I informed him before entering the carriage."

Grace opened her mouth to respond then clamped it shut. She was making this far too amusing.

"You shall just have to be patient and wait until we arrive." He glanced out the side window and scanned the street corner for the signs. "And we only have two more blocks to go." Andrew quirked one eyebrow. "Surely, you can wait that long, can't you?"

"Of course I can." She squared her shoulders and jutted her chin up an inch or two. "I am not a child."

No, she definitely wasn't that. As soon as she shifted her attention out the window, Andrew took that opportunity to observe her at greater length. Dressed in a simple, yet elegant striped blouse of pale blue with skirt to match and a wide, black velvet belt, she appeared every bit the lady he knew her to be, all the way up to her charming yet jaunty hat. To him, it seemed a bit overdone with all that lace, netting, flowers, and feathers, but the colors matched quite nicely. And it set off her eyes to perfection. Eyes that could drive him to his knees or give him strength to conquer any obstacle in his path.

He touched his own wool tweed then glanced at his plain pullover work shirt and trousers, and his grin became a frown. Why would she be willing to be seen in public with him, let alone even speak with him? No longer sporting his pinstripe trousers, wingtip shirt, vest, and coat, Andrew felt like an imposter in workman's clothes. He lowered his hand to where his silk puff tie normally graced his neck. Gone, too.

The carriage slowed to a stop, and Andrew looked out the window. "We're here," he announced and immediately exited to the sidewalk.

Andrew gripped the handle to the door and closed his eyes. He might not look the part, but he could still conduct himself as the gentleman his parents had raised him to be. Grace at least deserved that, and so much more.

"Andrew?"

Grace's concerned voice stirred him from his thoughts. He looked up at her and forced a brightness he didn't feel.

"I'm sorry," he said, offering her his hand.

She took it and stepped down in one fluid motion, bestowing a demure smile on him as she paused for him to close the door.

"Well?" Andrew swung his arm wide, gesturing toward the shop in front of them.

She looked at the windows first then raised her gaze to the sign above. "Adams Variety Store?" Grace returned her eyes to him. "This is the place you wanted to bring me? But why?"

Andrew had practiced what he'd say over and over in his head until he'd perfected his response. But now that he was standing in front of the store with her, words failed him.

"I…uh…"

Perfect. She stood there waiting for a reply, and he could only stutter. He had to pull himself together.

"I made a stop earlier today," he finally managed. "And I spoke to a gentleman who recommended we come here to search for those treasured books you lost." Andrew looked down and mumbled, "Thanks to me."

But she didn't seem to notice that last part. Instead her eyes widened and her entire visage brightened. She looked from him to the store to him and back to the store again. Like a young girl who'd just been presented with a brand-new pony for her birthday, Grace's excitement was almost tangible.

She covered his hands with hers. "Oh, Andrew, really?"

Andrew wanted to look down at their hands, but she might realize what she'd done and remove them. So instead, he shrugged. "This place is known for their diverse collection of goods of all kinds. Everything and anything a person might need. Dry goods, boots and shoes, carpets, window shades, books, furniture, and an endless variety of games and toys for children. If they don't have them, they are sure to at least know where else we might search."

"Thank you!" Grace leaned in so fast to place a kiss on his cheek, he didn't have time to react. She pulled away almost before he even realized what had happened. "This is perfect."

Before he could catch himself, Andrew glanced down at their hands, and Grace immediately did the same. Uh-oh. Just what he didn't want to do. She started to pull away, but he flipped his hands around to swap places with hers. Her head snapped up, and surprise registered in her eyes.

"You are quite welcome," he said softly, giving her hands a slight squeeze. "It is the least I can do after the loss I caused both you and your aunt."

A passerby looked at the two of them and then at their joined hands before continuing on his way. Grace noticed and her appreciation for Andrew's thoughtful gesture changed to wariness. They *were* standing on a busy and rather public city street. He'd best not draw any further attention to them than he already had. He released his hold and put a few extra inches between them. She quickly reached for her belt and gave it a tug then smoothed down her already wrinkle-free blouse.

"I would apologize for any untoward behavior on my part," he began then smirked. "But I rather liked the show of gratitude," he added with a wink.

Grace ducked her head as a shade of pink rivaling one of the prize roses in his mother's garden crept into her cheeks. Andrew probably shouldn't tease her, but he couldn't resist. And she made it so easy. Still, he didn't want to push beyond her comfort level. Extending an arm out toward the front doors, he offered the most encouraging smile he could muster.

"Shall we?"

She slowly raised her head and regarded first him then the store. With a nod, she took a step in the right direction. "I believe we shall."

Andrew placed his hand at the small of her back and guided her inside. Let the tongues wag and the whispers float on the air at the mismatched pair they made. He had the good fortune to be escorting a beautiful young lady, and her trust in him made him believe he *had* donned his finest attire. He had no reason to feel inferior.

* * *

After a disappointing visit to the Adams' store, they spent the remainder of the afternoon following one recommendation after another, combing the other bookshops in town, asking with all the broker establishments, and even checking with one or two specialty stores who had regular dealings with frequent merchandise providers. All to no avail.

Andrew had to clench his fists each time the hope in Grace's eyes turned to dejection with the negative response of a proprietor or broker. Every fiber in him itched to pull her close and ease her despair, but he couldn't. He just didn't like seeing that look in her eyes.

As they returned to the carriage following yet another dead end, Grace paused before stepping inside. "One moment," she said.

His hand remained in midair, waiting for her to accept his help into the carriage. She had one laced-up boot on the step but turned partway toward him.

"I cannot do this anymore." The words came out so quiet, Andrew had to strain to hear. "I know we still have some valuable advice on where else to search, but I'm not sure I can continue." Her shoulders slumped. "My aunt did this for over a year, and I can barely last one afternoon."

Again, the temptation to reassure her almost made his arms shake. But since he couldn't touch her, he could use words.

"I have an idea." He waited for her to look him in the eyes to be certain he had her attention. "Let's return to the shipyard, and you can deliver those papers to your uncle. I'll check with some of the merchants and tradesmen at the docks. They see a passel of goods come and go in their daily activities. I'll see if they know anything that might be helpful."

Grace chewed on her lower lip. Her eyes had lost that spark he'd come to expect, and the way she stood showed her weariness. Still, she managed to perk up a bit and give him a wan smile.

"Very well. If you believe it will be beneficial, I am willing to accept anything."

Taking his proffered hand, she again moved to enter the carriage. After she joined Harriet on the one side, Andrew climbed in and sat opposite her. Everyone remained silent for the entire ride, but that suited him just fine. Grace might not wish to continue the search, but he would. And maybe it would be better if he only notified her on the solid leads, instead of the loose trails that led them nowhere.

He glanced across the small space between them. She sat with her hands folded primly in her lap, the satchel she'd retrieved from the insurance company securely under her clasp. Perhaps a new topic of conversation would help.

"What is it your uncle had you fetch for him? I gather by the way you keep it close it's some rather important papers."

Grace looked up, somewhat startled by his sudden question, but also seeming a little relieved. "He has a meeting with the partners and investors tomorrow, and he needs these papers for that." She shrugged. "I don't know anything more."

No doubt a reassessment of their capital and where best to utilize the insurance coverage so it remained over the most valuable aspects of the business. Andrew had been privy to several conversations along those lines with his own father and their mill. Never a fun meeting, but a necessary one.

"Well, then we best get them to him as soon as we can." With a grin he added, "He no doubt already believes we've gotten lost somewhere."

Grace answered with a small smile of her own. "This might be the last time he sends me on an errand for him. We've been gone all afternoon."

"If he is cross in any way, let me explain. I've already been on the wrong side once." He straightened and assumed a tough and confident air. "I can handle it."

A giggle escaped her lips. "Better you than me."

In no time at all, they had arrived back at the shipyard. Matthew hopped down to assist Grace and Harriet, so Andrew merely descended after them. Grace glanced up the hill toward her uncle's office and said a few words to Harriet, who immediately headed toward the brick building. A moment later, Grace faced him.

"I wanted to thank you again for accompanying me today and for leading me on this impromptu expedition." She sighed. "Even if our efforts weren't successful, I do believe some progress was made."

"Yes. We now know where *not* to go next time."

He intended the remark to be lighthearted, but she didn't take it that way.

"A venture you shall be making alone, I am afraid." She closed her eyes for a few seconds and shook her head before her eyes opened again. "I need a rest from it for now."

Andrew reached out and tipped up her chin with his forefinger. "Hey," he said almost in a whisper, "I know today was difficult for you, but I'm not going to give up." He placed his thumb just below her mouth, fighting hard not to brush her lower lip. "I will not quit until those books are returned. I promise."

Her lower lip trembled, and she pulled it between her teeth. "Thank you," she managed with a shuddering breath.

His eyes drifted to her mouth. He swallowed twice. "My pleasure," he ground out before releasing her chin and stepping back. Distance. He needed distance.

Grace hesitated, her eyes taking on a sad and vulnerable expression. No, please. If she didn't leave right now, he might follow through on his desire to sample the soft enticement of her lips. A moment later she sighed and slowly turned toward the path. He almost reached out and spun her back around to face him, but he held himself in check.

Andrew marched away from her and down toward the docks. He'd inquire with the merchant sailors and tradesmen as he'd promised. And then maybe he'd take a cool dip in the river.

Chapter 15

"Good afternoon. My name is Montgomery T. Wentworth. Is Mr. Baxton by any chance available?"

The unfamiliar voice at the front door caught Grace's attention as she tucked the latest issue of *Lippincott's Monthly Magazine* under her arm and crossed the foyer on her way upstairs to fetch a shawl. An unknown caller on Saturday? They didn't often have them. She paused with one hand on the banister and attempted to peer around Harrison to catch a glimpse of the gentleman who'd come to call.

"I do apologize," the visitor continued, "for not announcing my arrival beforehand, but I have a matter of great import to discuss with him."

"I shall inform the master of your request," Harrison replied in his predictable monotone manner. "You may wait in the sitting room."

Harrison swung the door wide and in stepped a very

well-dressed gentleman with impeccable taste in clothing. Grace stepped back and pressed herself against the
railing. His satin-trimmed, dapper gray coat fastened
with polished buttons over a bluebird jacquard vest com-
plemented his dark gray pinstriped pants, which fell over
shiny black lace-up boots. Sliding her gaze upward again,
she noticed his finely folded silk puff tie held down with
what appeared to be a pearly tie tack. And the view only
improved from there.

She should duck back into the hallway to avoid being
seen, but the man arrested her attention. She couldn't
move. About Andrew's age, or perhaps a little older,
his angled jawline gave way to smooth cheekbones and
somewhat thin lips. He handed his silver plated cane
to Harrison and removed his felt derby hat, revealing a
wavy head of russet walnut hair, trimmed with precision
around his ears and allowed to grow slightly long at his
nape. That left the dark, brooding eyes that held just a
hint of arrogance.

And those eyes now turned on her.

With a slow and partial bow, his gaze never leaving
hers, the gentleman's thin lips turned into a smile. "Good
day to you, Miss…?"

Harrison's face registered annoyance, and with a stony
expression, he supplied, "This is Miss Grace Baxton, the
master's niece, sir. Miss Grace, this is Mr. Montgomery
Wentworth." With a stiff nod, Harrison went in search
of his employer.

Mr. Wentworth reached for her hand, bowing as he
raised it nearly to his mouth. "Miss Baxton, the pleasure
is all mine, I assure you."

His warm breath fanned her knuckles. Grace's left
arm went slack at the smooth tone of his cultured voice.
The magazine she held slipped with a rustling of pages

and slapped against the floor. As she bent to retrieve it, the gentleman stayed her with a gold-ringed hand and released her fingers.

"Allow me, please."

Still shaken, Grace took note of his finely manicured hands as he retrieved and dusted off her magazine. Now this was a gentleman. She admired the tailored fit of his coat and the high-stand collar of his dress shirt under his vest.

Straightening, Mr. Wentworth flashed a disarming smile and glanced down at the magazine before handing it to her.

"Ah, *Lippincott's*." He nodded toward the cover story. "And *The Picture of Dorian Gray*. A rather scintillating tale of the craving for personal satisfaction and a decadent lifestyle." His eyebrows arched. "I am surprised a lady such as yourself would find this story to your liking."

It wasn't the first time someone questioned her choice of literature, and it wouldn't be the last. Grace pressed the magazine against her chest and hitched her chin to look him straight in the eye.

The story hadn't ranked among her favorites, but it presented a unique perspective. "If I limit my reading, I limit my ability to form my own opinions, and therefore deprive myself of an experience that might broaden my horizons."

Wentworth placed a conciliatory hand across his coat lapels. "I consider myself duly chastised." He dipped his head. "Forgive my presumption. I am afraid my lapse of good manners has offended you. I am sorry."

Lapse? He'd been nothing short of flawless in his demeanor. His commanding presence and self-assured air differed from the other pompous gentlemen she met who dressed in similar fashion. On the contrary, Mr. Went-

worth seemed every bit the type of gentleman she re-
spected.

"So, is your business with my uncle of a personal or
professional nature?"

"Why don't we allow Mr. Wentworth to address the
answer of that question to me?" Uncle Richard announced
from behind Grace.

She spun to face her uncle. How long had Harrison
been gone? Had Mr. Wentworth distracted her that much?

Uncle Richard extended his hand in greeting as soon
as he reached them. "Richard Baxton," he said, drawing
his eyebrows together. "And Montgomery Wentworth,
is it?"

"Yes. An honor, sir." Wentworth shook her uncle's
hand. "Reports of your business acumen have spread far
and wide in this area. It is a distinct privilege to make
your acquaintance."

"I am sorry, Uncle." Grace spoke low and dipped her
head. "I didn't mean to pry."

Her uncle brushed a knuckle down her cheek and
smiled. "I know you didn't, Grace." He turned toward
their guest. "But I am curious about the purpose of your
visit, Mr. Wentworth. Would you like to accompany me
to my study? Or would the parlor perhaps be a more suitable room?"

"Actually…" Wentworth glanced at Grace. "My purpose involves your charming niece and the lady of the
house as well."

"Now you *do* have me intrigued." Her uncle tapped
his finger to his chin. "Please proceed."

"Perhaps showing you would be better than trying to
explain." He reached inside his coat pocket and retrieved
a rectangular package wrapped in simple brown paper

tied with twine. "I do believe this belongs to you, Miss Baxton," he said, handing the item to her.

Grace looked to her uncle, who nodded. She accepted the package, furrowing her brow as she touched the string. What could this gentleman have that belonged to her, and that made him come to their home to deliver it? She inhaled a sharp breath and widened her eyes. Oh! No, it couldn't be. Could it?

"If you open the package, Miss Baxton," Wentworth continued with a self-satisfied smile, "I believe all your questions will be answered."

Had he read her thoughts? Grace dropped her magazine onto the stairs next to her, yanked on the twine around the package, and peeled back the paper. She gasped. Yes! Oh, she couldn't believe it. The paper fell to the floor as she hugged the treasured book to her chest. The first edition copy of *Robinson Crusoe* had come home again. Grace lowered the book and flipped open the cover. There, in slightly faded ink sat the familiar words of her aunt's grandmother, five generations back.

"This book has produced the reaction I imagined it would," Wentworth said, his grin evident in his words.

Oh! Her manners! She'd forgotten them. Taking her eyes off the book for a moment, she looked up at their guest.

"Mr. Wentworth, thank you. This means more to me than words can say." She bestowed a bright smile upon him. "How did you find this? Where did you find this? And how did you know it belonged to us?"

Uncle Richard laughed. "One question at a time, Grace. I know you are overjoyed, but do allow our guest the opportunity to explain everything on his own before you belabor him with questions." Her uncle shifted his attention to Wentworth. "Before you do though, I would like to sincerely thank you for returning this item to us. My wife will be extremely pleased as well."

Wentworth clasped his hands behind him and rocked back and forth on his heels. "You are more than welcome, sir. It was a fortuitous circumstance that brought this book to my attention. As I said upon our introduction, sir, you are quite well-known in Wilmington and nearby towns." He scowled. "Your unfortunate experience with the reprobate, swindling thief became known in certain circles, as did the items you lost."

Grace bristled at the callous reference to Andrew. But of course, Mr. Wentworth didn't know him. Their guest's impression could only be based on hearsay. Had she been in his shoes, she might view the situation in a similar fashion. Truth be told, she *had* viewed things that way…at first.

"I believe there are three other titles which belong to you as well," Wentworth continued. "But I do not have them with me." His expression grew slightly smug. "I did take the liberty of asking the proprietor who has them for sale to hold them for me until I could speak with you. At my first opportunity, I shall return there and bring those books to you."

A nagging thought flitted through Grace's mind at the apparent convenience of Mr. Wentworth's story, but she brushed it away. She had her beloved book back. And it had been delivered by a rather charming and handsome gentleman. Nothing else mattered.

"Well, Mr. Wentworth," her uncle replied, "we are in your debt."

Wentworth waved off Uncle Richard's gratitude. "Think nothing of it. I would however like to discuss another business matter with you." He pulled one hand from behind his back and held it out in front of him. "But only if you can spare the time. If need be, I can leave my calling card, and you can get in touch with me at your earliest convenience."

So smooth. So refined. And with such manners. Grace became more impressed by the minute.

"Nonsense," Uncle Richard replied. "Come, come. Join me in my study, and we can discuss whatever you would like."

"If you don't mind, sir, I shall join you posthaste." He offered a kind smile to Grace before returning his attention to her uncle. "I should like to speak with your niece for a brief moment first."

Her uncle nodded. "Very well. But don't take long. I have an errand in about one hour."

The look her uncle gave Wentworth just before departing said quite a lot. Grace would have giggled had the silent warning not been so serious. Their guest better be on his best behavior.

"Miss Baxton," the gentleman began, "I am pleased to see you so delighted to hold that book in your hands once more."

"You have done me and my family a great service by bringing this book to me and letting us know the others will soon be back in their rightful place as well." She smiled. "As my uncle said, we are in your debt."

"And again, it is my pleasure." One side of his mouth curled up. "Although in your case, if I may be so bold, I might decide to collect on that debt in the form of a walk in the park."

Movement behind Wentworth's shoulder made her look in that direction. Just as quickly as her smile toward Wentworth had formed, it faltered. Andrew approached from the opposite corridor with a dark and brooding countenance that made her heart jump.

Had something happened below-stairs with another one of their servants? She tried to catch his eye, but he didn't even notice.

No. His attention was focused on Wentworth. The unconcealed contempt in his eyes could have wilted a flower. Could he possibly know something untoward about Mr. Wentworth? She prayed not. At last Andrew looked in her direction, seeming to struggle in his attempt to soften his expression. A lost cause.

"Grace," he said between clenched teeth, causing Wentworth to turn around in surprise, "if you're ready, Matthew has the carriage waiting. We can be on our way." He extended his hand and silently invited her to step toward him.

"Good day," Wentworth spoke up, offering his hand. "The name is Montgomery T. Wentworth. And you are...?"

Usually cordial and considerate, Andrew stared sullenly at Wentworth's extended hand as though it were leprous. That sort of oafish behavior would be more than welcome with the likes of some of the dock workers, but not with someone like Mr. Wentworth.

Grace reached out and lightly touched her guest's sleeve, eager to make amends. "Mr. Wentworth, please forgive me. I fear my excitement over the treasure you have returned has addled my wits. Allow me to introduce one of my uncle's employees, Mr. Andrew Bradenton."

"Mr. Bradenton," Wentworth repeated and extended his hand once more, a trace of smugness in his tone.

To Grace's embarrassment, Andrew still hesitated a fraction of a second before accepting the handshake, long enough for Grace to know he only did it out of deference to her. "Mr. Wentworth," he said, stepping in front of

Grace as if drawing boundaries. And he was marking her clearly off limits.

Men!

Grace stepped around Andrew, eager to move away before he made a further buffoon of himself. "It was a pleasure to make your acquaintance, Mr. Wentworth. Perhaps we'll meet again sometime." She bent to retrieve her magazine from the stairs as Andrew reached for her arm.

"I believe I am ready, Andrew," she announced, holding the book and magazine close and stepping away.

"Perhaps I can invite you out for that walk Wednesday next?" Wentworth called after her.

To be seen on the arm of such a dashing gentleman? How could she say no? Grace turned to answer. "Why, yes. I would like that very much." The muscles in Andrew's arm flexed against her fingers, but she ignored it. "Please come for me around half past ten. I shall be waiting."

Mr. Wentworth touched his thumb and forefinger to his forehead and bowed again. "Then, I shall see you Wednesday. It was a pleasure to meet you both. Good day."

No sooner had Wentworth stepped down the hall leading to her uncle's study when Andrew tugged her toward the front door as though hounds nipped at his heels. Gathering her skirts with her free hand, she nearly stumbled into him.

He remained silent all the way to the door and outside as they descended the front steps to the paved walk. He'd been given the day off because her uncle worked from home that day. And he'd invited her to a speech in the park. But now she wasn't sure she wanted to go.

"And just what was the meaning of that ill-mannered

exchange?" she demanded, breathless in her attempt to keep up with his pace.

He slowed momentarily, but didn't stop. "I don't wish to talk about it. You wouldn't understand."

"I wouldn't—"

Andrew stopped and spun to face her, heading off her impending outburst. "Grace, please." His words were minced through his even white teeth. "Trust me." With that, he whirled again and pulled her along toward the waiting carriage.

Trust him? How could she trust someone she didn't understand…especially after he'd behaved in such an oafish manner? And now he wouldn't even give her the courtesy of explaining himself? But, why would he—

As soon as they stopped, a single answer entered her mind. No, that wasn't possible. Was it? Grace took a deep breath, her thoughts staggering as fast as her heartbeat. Could he have been…jealous? Upset at Mr. Wentworth's attention? He hadn't acted that way toward anyone else she'd met. Why Wentworth?

She tried to see his face, to look into his telling eyes, but he kept his gaze averted and his head turned away. If she could be face-to-face with him, she'd know.

Only last night, Grace had started to see Andrew in a new light, especially considering his willingness to go to such great lengths in locating the books she'd lost. Now he didn't have to search anymore. She wanted to share the great news with him, but now didn't seem to be the best time. Could he possibly return some of those same feelings she'd only just started to experience? That might explain some of his actions.

Her head swam in confusion as Andrew assisted her into the carriage in cold silence. Just when she thought she was beginning to understand, his actions contradicted what she'd reasoned in her mind.

Would she ever figure out Andrew and his intentions?

Chapter 16

Andrew could have sworn that man looked familiar. But he couldn't place him. Not even the name registered as anyone he might know. Something about his swarthy appearance and slick talk nagged at Andrew though. The man was just too smooth. In both his story about finding the book and the way he'd conducted himself in front of Grace and her uncle.

And that book.

The one no one in any shop in Wilmington had seen. Not even the merchant sailors and tradesmen at the docks could tell him much of anything. Yet in walked this stranger, brandishing not only the one missing book, but saying he had located all four of them. Then to request a private audience with Mr. Baxton? It didn't add up.

No, he shouldn't have eavesdropped on their entire conversation. And Grace would be quite disappointed if she knew. Ah yes, Grace. The young woman he'd invited to the park now sat opposite him, glowering. He had been quite the cad. He really should apologize.

"Grace?"

Nothing. Not even a twitch indicating she'd heard him.

"Grace, please," Andrew tried again.

If things between them were different, he'd move to the seat beside her and take her hands in his. But that would likely earn him a menacing glare and a firm strike on the arm at this point. Besides, she'd introduced him to Wentworth as nothing more than one of her uncle's employees. Not even as a friend. No, he'd be safer if he remained where he sat, holding his felt hat in his lap to prevent his hands from doing anything they shouldn't. And he'd try one more time. Third time lucky?

"Grace, I would like to apologize…if you will allow me to do so." More silence as she continued to stare out the window. "And the apology would go much smoother if you would at least look in my direction." He made an attempt at humor, hoping that might break through her silent wall. "I would prefer not to speak to the seat cushions, despite their charm."

That did it. Finally a spark of a reaction. Andrew schooled his facial features into a somber and contrite expression. If she caught him grinning, it'd all be over.

Slowly Grace shifted in her seat and angled toward him. She slowly turned her head and opened her heavily lidded eyes to regard him. Andrew flinched. Maybe he should have left her staring out the window. It would have been better than the contempt he read in her eyes at that moment. But he'd already started this. He couldn't back down now.

"I really am sorry," he began. "And you were right. My manners were deplorable. I don't know what came over me, except that Wentworth fellow grated on my nerves.

Something doesn't seem quite right with him." He leaned forward and implored, "Forgive me? Please?"

Andrew sat like a statue, waiting for her reply. He held his breath and fought hard to keep his leg from bouncing or his foot from tapping. Let her say something soon.

"Very well," she finally said.

His breath came out in a whoosh, and his shoulders relaxed.

"But this doesn't repair all the damage you've done," she warned. "It is a good thing my uncle wasn't standing there to witness your behavior, or he might have had some choice words to say to you." The look she gave him next reminded him of the schoolteacher he'd had at the academy nearly fifteen years ago. "But I suppose I can keep this between us for now…as long as you promise it won't happen again."

"Thank you," he replied. "And I promise."

Well, that had gone far better than he'd imagined. Good thing she didn't seem to be one to hold grudges or their time together would be nothing but stilted. At least now he could look forward to attending the public speech with her and being seen accompanying such a lovely young lady.

"Now, perhaps you will allow me to compliment you on the fetching gown you've chosen this afternoon?" He sighed and gave her a sheepish grin. "I had intended to say so before, but well, you saw how that played out."

A trace of a grin played at her rosy mouth—a mouth that shouldn't be distracting him at the moment. He forced his gaze upward to meet her eyes and smiled at the glinting amusement he saw there.

"Thank you, Andrew." Grace smoothed one hand across the ruffled lace bordering her blouse buttons then fluffed out her skirt a bit. "Aunt Charlotte helped me select this ensemble. I had a more simple walking dress in mind."

"Then I shall be certain to thank your aunt the next time I see her."

Perhaps for more reasons than one. If her aunt had encouraged Grace to change her mind, Mrs. Baxton might be encouraging something else between him and her niece. Only time would tell.

Andrew stretched his long legs, angling them off to the side, and leaned back against the cushions. Interlocking his fingers behind his head, he regarded Grace through narrowed eyes.

"Now, tell me more about this recent treasure you've acquired," he said with a grin and a wink as he nodded toward the book on the seat next to her.

Grace brightened considerably at this. "How did you know?"

He shrugged. "Never let it be said that I don't pay attention."

"Or eavesdrop," she retorted with a giggle.

"That, too." He smiled. "What's the story behind this book? You're going to have to start at the beginning."

She launched into the tale of the book that had become a precious commodity to her and her family, and Andrew settled in against the seat. Her face reflected her joy, and her demeanor bubbled with enthusiasm. He didn't want to think it was due to Wentworth and the part he'd played in returning the book. Even that couldn't dampen his enjoyment of the moment. Sitting opposite her, free of a shadowing lady's maid for the first time, Andrew looked forward to what was yet to come.

This made it all worthwhile.

* * *

Wentworth again.

That was the third time in the past week the man had come to the shipyards to escort Grace on a walk. Andrew seethed and clenched his teeth as Wentworth placed a hand at the small of Grace's back and urged her forward. If only Grace didn't respond to him with such enthusiasm, it might make seeing them together a bit more bearable. But no. She graced him with a beaming smile and dropped everything in order to accompany him the moment he asked. Andrew leaned over the railing of the ship, trying to get a better view of the pair.

"What's the matter, Bradenton?" James clapped him on the shoulder, startling him from his irritated thoughts and nearly causing him to drop his hammer in the river. "Got yourself a case of the green sickness?"

"No." The last thing he needed was someone else noticing his jealousy. He attempted to brush off his interest in Grace and Wentworth with a shrug. "What makes you say that?"

"Oh…just that I called your name four times before I had to walk over here and find out what had your attention." He paused to take a breath. "Since it obviously isn't your work."

Andrew jerked his head around. "I'm sorry. I'll focus."

"See that you do." James nodded in the direction Grace and Wentworth had gone. "And do your spying on your own time from now on."

Andrew growled at himself. He had to pull it together. Grace could take walks with whomever she pleased. Andrew had no claim on her. Not an official one anyway. Anything between them clearly only existed in his mind. So why did Wentworth aggravate him so much? It was right there in front of him. Andrew knew it. Right there for the taking, and he couldn't put his finger on it.

Then it hit him.

Yes! That was it. Andrew straightened. He knew where he'd seen the man before. But wait. If that were true, then Wentworth's presence meant more than merely preventing Grace from spending time with Andrew. The blackguard was up to something else far more sinister. But how could he prove it?

"Miss Baxton, your company this afternoon made the walk doubly enjoyable." Wentworth bowed over Grace's hand and placed a chaste kiss on her knuckles. "I appreciate your willingness to accept my invitation without my notifying you beforehand."

Andrew clenched his fists and swallowed at the smooth-as-honey tone of the man's voice. If he didn't release Grace's hand, he might find it shoved away. But Grace withdrew her own hand and reached into her reticule for a fan, which she snapped open and waved in front of her face. Andrew couldn't tell if she was warding off the early-August heat or being coquettish. Or both. He hoped it was the former.

"Mr. Wentworth, you make each and every walk most pleasurable."

"Then, might I invite you to accompany me to Sunday services three days hence?"

Grace nodded and continued to fan herself rapidly. "You may. And I accept."

"I shall call for you around nine."

"Very good," she replied. "I look forward to it."

Another bow. "Not as much as I."

Andrew waited for Grace to disappear inside the brick

building. When Wentworth was a decent distance away from the shipyard office, Andrew approached.

"I'd like a word with you, Wentworth."

The man paused and turned in a slow arc, his expression one of annoyed tolerance. "I beg your pardon...Bradenton, is it?"

"Don't play that game with me." Andrew held back a groan. "You know very well who I am and how I came to be here. Don't act like our supposed introduction two weeks ago was genuine."

Wentworth sighed. His eyes registered disinterest, and his thin lips were pressed into a nonchalant line. "I see you finally put two and two together," he replied with grating arrogance. "I had wondered if you would recognize me or if you had even seen me that night your foolish decision led you down this dreadfully unfortunate path."

Andrew wanted to punch that self-righteous smirk off the man's face. But what good would that do except make him feel better? No, he wouldn't give Wentworth the satisfaction of seeing him lose control. He was here for Grace's sake, and for her family as well. He had to keep reminding himself of that.

"I did see you, and while I didn't recognize you right away, I do now." Andrew took one step closer to Wentworth and looked him in the eye. "And I'm warning you," he ground out. "Stay away from Grace and stay away from Hannsen & Baxton Shipping."

"Or what?" The man laughed. "Don't tell me you'll seek me out to enact whatever form of revenge you might concoct. Because if that's the case, I believe I have no reason to be concerned."

How could the man be so conceited as to think he actually stood a chance should Andrew decide to let go of his restraint? He might stand a whole inch taller, but what he had in height, he lacked in build. Something in Wentworth's eyes told Andrew not to press though. And he didn't.

"If anything happens to Grace or her family, if you hurt her in any way…" Andrew clenched his fists again. "I'll expose you for the scoundrel you are."

Wentworth shrugged. "Be my guest," he replied. "Tell Miss Baxton of your suppositions. Or better yet, inform Mr. Baxton himself. Neither of them will believe you. Of that, I'm certain." He sighed and raised his right hand to inspect his nails, as if the conversation bored him. "Now, if you are finished, I shall return to more important matters that require my attention."

Andrew wanted to say more, but now was not the time or the place. He couldn't leave Wentworth with the last word though.

"I'll be watching you," he said with as much menace as he could muster.

Another grating laugh. "I wouldn't have it any other way," Wentworth retorted and walked away.

Andrew almost ran after him to give him the pummeling he deserved. But he didn't. That pent-up anger had to come out though. With a feral growl he swung and punched the storage shack to his left. The wood cracked and splintered and searing pain turned his knuckles to fire. Ouch! Not the wisest move.

"What was that all about?"

Andrew stiffened at Grace's voice behind him.

"Grace!"

Had she heard what he and Wentworth had said? He certainly hoped not.

"How long have you been standing there?"

"Long enough to see you enter into a boxing match

with an innocent shed," she replied. "Would you care to tell me what's wrong?"

Andrew massaged his throbbing hand and turned to face her, forcing his anger to some faraway spot. She didn't deserve to be the recipient of his repressed hostility. In all honesty, she hadn't done anything wrong. But how was he going to tell her that?

"Wentworth and I had a few things to discuss. And the conversation didn't go exactly as I had planned." At least that wasn't a lie.

Grace narrowed her eyes, clearly not convinced by his explanation. She peered over his shoulder in the direction Wentworth had gone then returned her gaze to him. She reached for his injured hand and raised it for her inspection. "A conversation that led you to punch a shack?" She pressed her lips into a thin line and sighed. "Somehow I find that rather difficult to believe." Releasing his hand, she quirked an eyebrow. "Care to tell me the truth?"

With one look in her eyes, he couldn't lie. Andrew closed his eyes and prayed for strength.

"I discovered something about Mr. Wentworth and warned him to stay away from you."

She chuckled. "Whyever would you do that?" She waved her hand idly in the air. "Mr. Wentworth poses no threat."

That's what she thought. "Don't be so certain," he countered. "The man is up to no good." Andrew reached for her hands and compelled her to focus on him. "I promise you, Grace. You need to be careful around him."

Grace pulled her hands free and laughed off his warning. "Don't be silly, Andrew. You are merely imagining things that aren't there. And what's worse, you're acting like a jealous schoolboy."

He groaned. Why wouldn't she listen to reason? "I am

not jealous," he retorted, hearing the anger in his own words. "I have no reason to be." And *there* was the lie.

Grace stepped back as though he'd struck her. The carefree expression on her face turned to one of distress and hurt. Moisture welled in her eyes, and her lower lip trembled. But she stood resolute. A moment later, she whirled away from him and disappeared around the side of the building.

Andrew wanted to kick himself. He'd intended to caution her, to make her aware of Wentworth's schemes. But he'd only succeeded in wounding her...far deeper than if he'd physically lashed out at her. She definitely wouldn't listen to him now. He could only pray she'd reconsider what he'd said *before* his outburst. Otherwise, he'd have to be there to pick up the pieces.

Chapter 17

Andrew shut the door behind him and crossed the lower courtyard to the stairs leading up to the back lawn. Maybe a breath of fresh air would help him clear his head and get his thoughts flowing in the right direction. Although the sun had set, the heat from the mid-August day remained.

Taking his lantern in one hand, Andrew reached into his shirt pocket for the match he'd stowed there on his way out the door. With a scratch against the stone, the match sizzled, and he lit the wick that ran down into the oil.

There had to be a way to prove Wentworth's underhanded involvement in everything. He'd tried to make a few inquiries on his own, but he'd come up dry. Maybe if he could figure out who employed the man, or what his intentions were regarding Mr. Baxton and the shipping business. If he could get a shred of evidence, he could take it to Mr. Baxton and encourage him to investigate further.

But how?

A branch snapped to Andrew's right. He froze. The hairs on the back of his neck stood up.

"Hello?" His voice sounded thin, even to his own ears. He cleared his throat. "Is somebody out there?"

Andrew turned toward a slight rustling in the bushes. He held up the lantern, but the light didn't extend far enough.

"Hello?" he tried again.

Only silence. Eerie silence.

Andrew took two more steps, but before he could take his third, the lantern was yanked from his hand and snuffed out. The sudden darkness set his nerves even more on edge. Of all the nights for a new moon, why'd it have to be tonight?

Scuffling boots on grass and dirt sounded around and behind him. He spun to the left and right. Whoever was there avoided his vision with adept agility. A second later two sets of beefy hands grabbed hold of his arms. Andrew fought against them, digging in his heels as they dragged him toward the stables.

Great. Maybe Jesse or Willie would be there and wake up. He prayed it'd be Jesse, although he'd take anyone at this point. Or did the two hands sleep in the house with the other servants?

Finally the two men stopped and a lone figure stepped out from the shadows.

"Wentworth," Andrew hissed. He pulled against his human restraints and got nowhere.

"Yes. I see you still remember my name," the man's taunting voice replied. "Although that doesn't come as a surprise, considering the many times you've mentioned me lately."

Andrew could see Wentworth's silver-plated cane, held about waist-high in the man's hands.

"It seems you've been asking about me quite a lot during the past couple weeks." Wentworth paced a short span back and forth in front of Andrew, tapping his cane into the palm of his left hand. "Tell me, did you find out what you wanted to know?"

Andrew wasn't going to play this man's game. He clenched his teeth to keep from hurling a few choice curse words in his direction.

Wentworth leaned closer and cupped his fingers to his right ear. "What's that? I don't believe I caught your reply."

Andrew writhed back and forth. But his assailants held tight, their grips never loosening.

A menacing laugh split the night air. "I wouldn't bother attempting to break free. My men here are the best at what they do. And you won't be escaping from them anytime soon."

The best at what they do? Andrew didn't even want to think about what Wentworth meant by that.

"See"—the man resumed his pacing across the small patch—"I have spent a great deal of time planning out my strategy where Baxton, his niece, and his shipping business are concerned. Your dire need a few months back played right into my plans, providing me with a stooge to incriminate and set my plan into action." He waved his left hand in the air. "And the other thefts in the same neighborhood only assured my anonymity."

Heat burned in Andrew's chest, and face. He couldn't believe he'd been a pawn in this man's schemes all along.

"But we can't have you poking your nose in places it

doesn't belong. You might stumble on to something important. Something that might bring to light all of my careful strategies." He tapped his cane. "So I brought along some insurance tonight. If you hadn't come outside when you did, I would've found a way to entice you outdoors." Wentworth paused in front of Andrew and bent toward him. "And now, I shall leave my men to deliver a final message to you to cease with your interference. I believe it will be most effective."

Before he realized what the two men had planned, a fist smashed squarely into the ridge of bone over Andrew's eye. White light flashed, and Andrew blinked. He'd been freed from his confines, but he could only stumble in the dark. His vision cleared just as one of the men came at him again.

Andrew charged and swung, but his adversary dodged him. Blood pounding in his temples, Andrew plowed into one of the men, and once again, the thug danced away. But not before delivering a stabbing kidney punch. Ignoring what felt like a steel blade twisting in his back, Andrew spun on the man with a powerful hook, only to have it deflected and his arm wrenched behind his back as he was driven to the ground.

That hadn't gone well.

Andrew didn't know if he'd blacked out or if he'd blocked out the full extent of the attack. Either way, only pain registered to his brain. It didn't feel like anything was broken, but with everything in a fog, he couldn't know for sure.

"Harlan ain't gonna like that we had to resort to this..."

The words of one of the thugs trailed off as his attackers disappeared into the night. Andrew's head rolled around on his neck. He stuck out his tongue and tasted blood. He should press his handkerchief to the cut, but his arms lacked the strength to pull the folded square of cotton from his pocket. The solid wall of support behind him meant he must be propped up against the side of the stables.

That was when the parting words of his assailant registered. Harlan. As in Harlan & Hollingsworth. At last! He had his shred of evidence.

Andrew's eyes drifted shut. He'd close his eyes for just a few minutes to regain his strength. Then he'd take his proof to Mr. Baxton.

"Andrew?"

Hesitant hands pressed against his chest and rocked him back and forth a little. He recognized that voice. It belonged to Bart, one of the footmen at the Baxton manor.

"Andrew, get up," Bart encouraged. "You have to get up. Mr. Baxton wants to see you in his study right away."

"Uhhh," Andrew moaned. Where was he? And how had he gotten from the stables to here? He turned his head toward the light coming in through the window and opened his eyes a slit. Daytime. But which day? Saturday or Sunday? Had one or two days passed? He had no idea.

"We did the best we could with your wounds," Matthew said. "But if anything's hurting that we can't see, there wasn't much we could do about it."

"And really, you don't look all that bad, all things considered," Marcus added.

Two footmen and the carriage driver. Who else knew about his unfortunate encounter that night?

"Relax," Marcus continued. "No one else knows you're up here but the three of us."

Andrew forced one eye fully open and squinted. The three other men stood like guardians at the foot and sides of the bed that had been his for the past three months. He had somehow been carried inside and up three flights of stairs without anyone else noticing? Amazing. With their help Andrew managed to swing his legs over the side of the bed and place his feet on the floor. His vision began to clear enough to focus on the room and the men around him. He gained strength with each deep breath he took.

The men had also given him a fresh change of clothes and washed away what he could only assume was dried blood. Mr. Baxton wanted to see him downstairs immediately? Maybe word had reached him of the attack on his property, and he wanted to see the proof for himself. But Marcus had just said no one else knew.

What could Mr. Baxton want with him? Only one way to find out.

Tapping into whatever strength reserves he could find, Andrew pushed himself to his feet and stumbled toward the door. He flexed as he walked, using the wood railing along the wall for support. Maybe his injuries weren't so bad after all. He touched a finger to his temple and winced. Rolling his shoulders produced the same result. Then again, maybe not. He wished he had a looking glass handy, so he could see if he looked as bad as he felt. No time for that though. He had to get downstairs.

A few minutes later, Andrew walked down the corridor toward the study. The hum of voices greeted him before he reached the door.

"No, I cannot believe it." Grace's voice reached him first. "Andrew would never do a thing like that."

"But he has stolen before." Mrs. Baxton's calm voice pointed out, reminding him that he might never escape that branding.

"That was a solitary incident," Grace again protested. "He's changed."

Andrew had no idea what had happened, but hearing Grace defend him bolstered his spirits and gave him strength to face whatever lay behind that door. With one hand on the smooth surface, Andrew pushed it open. The creak of the hinges announced his arrival.

All heads turned toward him. Grace gasped and Mrs. Baxton covered her mouth with her hand. Well, that answered one question. He obviously *did* look as bad as he felt.

"Jupiter, man!" Mr. Baxton was the first to respond. "What in the world happened to you?"

Andrew offered a rueful grin. "I fell into a couple of men's fists and came out on the losing end." He took a quick glance around the room to find the constable who'd been present at his sentencing and one other staff member standing back from the other four people gathered. "What's this all about?"

Mr. Baxton inhaled a long breath and released it slowly. His hands went behind his back. Uh-oh. That wasn't a good sign. "Andrew, there have been some rather important papers and some money that have gone missing from my safe here in this study."

A safe? He'd never seen one. Then again, this was only the second time he'd been in this room. Andrew furrowed his brow. "And what does that have to do with me?"

Something told him he already knew. He wouldn't have been called down here and the constable wouldn't be in this room if the answer were anything different than he supposed.

"The money was found stuffed in a drawer next to your bed," Mr. Baxton replied. "And one page of the papers was found at the bottom of your wardrobe. The rest of the papers are still missing."

Andrew sighed. Yet again. The victim of a carefully

thought-out plan. Wentworth's words came back to him. He'd said this warning would stick. And so it had.

"Who found the items in question?" He likely didn't want to know, but he had to ask anyway. Call it morbid curiosity.

"That would be Sebastian, here," Baxton answered.

Andrew leaned to the right to get a look at the man Baxton indicated. "Him!" Andrew pointed at the footman who'd just been identified. "He was here the night I first came to this house. He's the one who unlocked the rear door and granted me access."

Yet one more piece to the confusing puzzle his life had become of late.

"That's ridiculous," the young man protested. "It wasn't even my night to take watch on the main level."

"We've got no witnesses to your intrusion," the constable chimed in. "But that's all in the past. You've served your time for that mistake." He smoothed his fingers down his mustache. "Now there's substantial proof to incriminate you yet again. And I'm afraid we're going to have to take you to the jail until this can all be worked out."

Jail? For a crime he hadn't committed. Not a chance! That was just the first stop toward the penitentiary in Philadelphia. He'd avoided that place once. He didn't intend to tempt fate a second time.

"But I didn't do it! Surely you cannot believe I'd repay your generous trust in me with this kind of treachery, can you?"

Andrew searched the faces of everyone in the room. Sebastian certainly wouldn't be of any help. And neither would the constable. That left only Mr. Baxton, Mrs. Baxton, and Grace. He let his gaze fall on the latter.

She'd been defending him when he'd first arrived. Why was she remaining silent now?

"Please, Grace, you must believe me." Touching what he knew was a visible bruise on his face and then the cuts around his mouth, he continued. "Look at me. Why would I have been so brutally attacked and left to rot for the most part if I had stolen these things?"

"Maybe you were on your way out the door when someone caught you in the act," Sebastian chimed in.

"That is enough, Sebastian." Baxton's stern reprimand effectively silenced the lad.

"But if I was on my way out, why would I have stashed the items in my room where they could be found? Why did I not have them on me?"

His plight was likely a lost cause, but he had to try.

"Look." The constable adjusted his wire-rimmed spectacles and tugged at his overcoat lapels. "None of us here are saying it's an open-and-shut case. But we have to act on what we've found." The man's face turned grim. "And that means we have to take you in for further questioning. At least until we can get to the bottom of things."

The constable withdrew a pair of silver handcuffs. "I'm sorry to have to do this, son, but it's the law."

For a brief moment, Andrew thought of resisting, but in his present state, he wouldn't get far. No. Fighting would only lend credence to his presumed guilt. If he cooperated, maybe things wouldn't be so bad. But he wasn't about to stick out his hands willingly. He spotted a tablet of paper and a pencil on a round table near one of the wingback chairs. He snatched a single piece and the pencil and wrote down a few words before folding the paper into his palm.

After he returned the pencil to its previous spot, he caught Grace watching him with a question in her eyes.

The constable stepped toward him, and Andrew tensed. No time to explain.

"Grace, please. Look into this with an objective eye. Persuade your aunt and uncle to take on a further investigation," he pleaded and silently rejoiced when a bit of resolute strength shined back at him. "You said yourself you don't believe I did this. Now prove it. Please. That's all I ask."

"Hold out your hands please, Bradenton."

Andrew did as the constable asked, taking care to keep the note tucked under his fingers. When the handcuffs snapped around his wrists, he cringed. At least the last time he hadn't been led away in shackles. Somehow the bindings made the situation seem that much more hopeless.

"All right," the officer stated, "let's go."

When the constable moved to Andrew's other side and swung him around toward the door, he stepped near Mr. Baxton.

Andrew pleaded with his eyes for the man to understand. "I'm sorry," he said.

At first only a wall of disappointment reflected back at him from the dark depths. Then a spark of trust appeared. Perfect! A tiny morsel of hope. He didn't need anything more.

He tried to extend his hands closer to Baxton. Feigning a stumble, Andrew managed to take a step or two toward him. The man registered his surprise, but Andrew quickly shoved the paper into his hands before the constable could pull him away.

He prayed Baxton…and Grace, too…would investigate further.

Chapter 18

It couldn't be true. It just couldn't.

Grace had repeated those words to herself countless times over the past five days. Yet, no further evidence had come forth to prove otherwise. She folded her arms and rested them on the table. The veranda afforded her privacy while also allowing her to gaze out on the back lawn of her uncle's manor.

The groundskeeper and gardeners kept the plants, roads, paths, buildings, and orchard in pristine condition. From the plants lining the garden path to the berry patches and the peach, apple, and pear orchards at the rear of the property, every piece of the manor's grounds seemed to be laid out in perfect order.

Not everything *was* as it should be though. Andrew sat alone, awaiting his sentencing for a second time. Only this time, he'd spent almost a full week in a jail cell. A cold, lonely, barren jail cell. She had to do something. But what?

"Excuse me, Miss Grace?"

Grace searched the veranda for the owner of the meek voice. Finally her eyes fell on a young chambermaid who stood partially hidden by the stone wall and the rather substantial shrub at the opening to the lawn.

"You may approach, Ella."

The girl took a few shuffling steps before her entire body could be seen. Even then she refused to let go of the ornate planter that came nearly up to her waist.

"Ella, you have no reason to be afraid." Grace beckoned to her. "Please. Come and tell me what's on your mind."

Grace's encouragement seemed to work. Ella released her hold on the planter and closed the distance to where Grace sat, but she still maintained a respectful distance. Her eyes remained downcast, and she buried her fingers in the folds of her apron.

Would the maid ever get the gumption to speak? Grace didn't want to scare her off, but at this rate, it would be dinnertime before the girl managed to share her concerns. All of a sudden, Ella snapped up her head and inhaled a deep breath.

"I beg your pardon, Miss Grace, but I couldn't remain silent any longer," she said in a single breath.

"Silent, Ella?" Grace drew her eyebrows together. "Silent about what?"

"About Andrew, Miss Grace."

Andrew? Ella knew something about Andrew? Grace almost jumped up from her seat to beg Ella to continue. But at any moment the girl could bolt. And then Grace would have no idea what she'd come to say.

Calming both her breathing and her heartbeat, Grace

offered a reassuring smile to the girl. "Ella, please proceed when you're ready."

That minor boost must have given Ella the courage she needed. Her bowed posture straightened, and her averted gaze became direct.

"Miss Grace, I'm sorry I didn't come to you or Mrs. Baxton sooner, but I was worried Sebastian might find out and snitch on me, and then I might end up like Andrew."

"Snitch, Ella? To whom?"

"To Mr. Wentworth, miss. He was the one behind this whole thing. Sebastian knew I knew, and he threatened to report me to Mr. Wentworth if I said anything. So I kept my mouth shut." She took a bold step closer. "But I like Andrew, Miss Grace. And it isn't right to see him stuck in that jail when he's done nothing wrong."

Grace closed her eyes and took several calming breaths. She'd prayed every day that week for an answer, and now she had it. With a smile she opened her eyes and reached out toward the maid.

"Ella, please come and sit and tell me everything. I am certain my uncle will be quite interested in all that you have to say."

"Uncle Richard?"

Grace pushed on the partially open door and peeked inside the darker room.

"Come in, Grace, come in," her uncle replied.

She stepped all the way into the study and went straight to her uncle's desk. He stood behind it, sifting through some papers.

"Uncle Richard, we were wrong," she announced without preamble. They'd wasted more than enough time already.

Her uncle grabbed the stack and tapped it against the desk's surface, setting the papers in alignment. "Yes, Grace, we were."

Her eyes widened. "You knew?"

"I only discovered it earlier this morning." He raised the stack he held and flicked the top page with his fingers. "Thanks to this report…or rather answers to some of the inquiries I made this week."

"So you believed Andrew, too, didn't you?"

Grace didn't know why she'd doubted that. It was her uncle, after all, who forgave Andrew halfway through his sentence. And her uncle had trusted Andrew enough to employ him at the shipyards. Why wouldn't he believe Andrew?

"You remember that note Andrew scribbled right before the constable escorted him out?"

How could she forget? He'd seemed so intent about it, so determined to get it done. "Of course." Grace nodded.

"Well, he'd written the name of Harlan & Hollingsworth on it."

The shipping business just two blocks away from Hannsen & Baxton? "What did he mean by it? Or mean for you to find?"

"Turns out our Mr. Wentworth works for them, and he's been the key manipulator in a scheme to steal the blueprints for our newest iron-hulled ship." Her uncle set down the report on his desk again. "The bound stack of bills in the safe at the time were merely a bonus. And only part of it was planted in Andrew's room."

"Oh, Uncle, we have made such a grave mistake."

He sighed. "I know." Planting both palms flat on his desk, her uncle captured her in his direct gaze. "And I believe it's high time we set things right."

She smiled. "I couldn't agree more."

"But first…" He glanced over her shoulder and beckoned to someone who'd just arrived. He moved around
his desk to stand next to Grace. "I believe we should pray
for guidance on how to proceed and ask God's forgiveness for not doing right by Andrew."

Aunt Charlotte joined them, taking hold of both her
husband's and Grace's hands. "I think that is a truly
splendid idea."

The constable slammed the door closed on the jail
wagon with a self-satisfied smirk. He touched two fingers
to his double-brimmed hat and saluted before climbing
into the driver's seat and setting off for the jail.

Grace watched the wagon disappear behind one of the
many industrial buildings along the river. She shouldn't
be happy to see someone sent to prison, but Wentworth
had received his due comeuppance. Stepping an inch or
two closer to Andrew, Grace nudged him. He nudged
her in return, and she cast a sly smile up at him from the
corner of her eye.

"Well, well, well," Uncle Richard announced, a bit
louder than necessary. "Now that we have all that sorted
out, there are just two things that need to be settled."

Her uncle exchanged a private look with her aunt, and
they both smiled.

"Uncle Richard?" Just what were those two up to?

Richard reached behind his vest and withdrew an envelope. He tapped it against his left hand and pressed
his lips into a thin line as he addressed Andrew. Andrew squared his shoulders and distanced himself just
slightly from Grace.

"Andrew, my boy, you have more than proven yourself
at least three times over and endured far more than any
man should have to endure in your shoes." He glanced

again at his wife, who nodded and gave his arm a squeeze. "With that being said, Mrs. Baxton and I agreed we owed you more than just our words of gratitude."

"Sir, you don't need to—"

"Please don't attempt to dissuade me, my boy," Uncle Richard interrupted. "We have made up our minds, and"—he handed the envelope to Andrew—"this is yours."

Andrew didn't immediately reach for it, so Uncle Richard shook it in front of him.

"Don't force me to tuck it into your pocket as well," he threatened with a half grin.

"Andrew, he means what he says," Grace chimed in. "He'll do it, too."

With a sigh, Andrew accepted the gift. "Very well, but know that I do this under coercion from two very persuasive people."

Uncle Richard laughed. "I wouldn't have it any other way." He leveled a frank look at Andrew. "You be sure and put that to good use." Empathy entered his eyes. "Maybe even help pay for a surgery or two."

Andrew inhaled a shuddering breath. "I will, sir. Thank you."

Grace tucked her hand into the crook of Andrew's arm and leaned against him. She couldn't love her aunt and uncle more than at that very moment.

"And now about that other matter," her uncle said with a slight chuckle. "I wanted to tell you both that I give my permission for you, Andrew, to court my niece."

What? Grace straightened, looking from her uncle to her aunt to Andrew and back to her uncle again. Court her? Had Andrew somehow managed to speak to her uncle without her knowing?

Uncle Richard held up his hand. "Now, before you

both start speculating or asking a lot of questions, let me assure you no one has spoken to me or made any intentions verbally known." He clasped his wife's hand in his and placed his free arm around her waist, pulling her close. "I do however have eyes, and I know undisguised interest when I see it. So I'll save you both the trouble and grant my permission right from the start." He narrowed his eyes. "You treat her right, my boy."

Andrew reached out and shook her uncle's hand. "I will, sir. I promise."

Her aunt and uncle stepped close and each placed a kiss on Grace's cheek before they left her standing alone with Andrew. Moisture suddenly formed in Grace's palms, and she wiped them on her skirt. Andrew turned to face her, taking her now dry hands in his. He opened his mouth once, then twice, then shut it. Good to know she wasn't the only one having trouble coming up with something to say.

Finally he shrugged. "Guess your uncle pretty much said it all, huh?"

Oh, he wasn't going to get away that easily. And she intended to have her say as well. Giving him another sly smile, she allowed her delight at the recent turn of events to travel all the way to her eyes. "Not exactly," she replied with a wink.

He narrowed his eyes. "And just what is that supposed to mean?"

"Well." She drew out the word. "For starters, it means I still have to apologize to you for not believing you when you tried to warn me about Wentworth. I knew you weren't guilty of stealing those papers and money from the safe, but if I had listened to you from the start"—she reached up and caressed the bruise above his eye—"you might not have had to suffer to such a great extent." Returning her hand to his grasp, she raised her eyebrows. "Forgive me?"

Andrew gave her hands a squeeze. "Of course. You didn't even need to ask." He shrugged. "We all make mistakes. Who am I to judge?" He grinned. "Even if you did have the wool pulled over your eyes by a dapper, yet devious, rake."

Heat stole into her cheeks, and she dipped her head. He immediately reached to tilt her chin with his forefinger so she again met his gaze.

"Besides, after all that's been forgiven of me, how could I not in turn forgive you?" Andrew grinned. "I had a lot of time to think these past few days, sitting in that jail cell. And I talked a lot to God, too."

"What did you discuss?"

"God and I? We had some real quality one-on-one time." He gave her a rueful grin and ran his hand through his hair, making several of the thick strands stand on end. "And He set me straight on a few things, too."

Grace reached up to smooth out some of the haphazard locks, and when she lowered her hand, Andrew captured it again in his.

"Namely how carelessly I'd treated our friendship, and that I hadn't made it clear how I feel about you." His thumbs started making lazy circles on the backs of her hands. "But not anymore." He gave her hands another squeeze and pinned her in his earnest gaze. "Miss Grace Baxton," he heralded with great fanfare, "will you do me the honor of allowing me to come calling at your earliest convenience?"

A giggle started in her stomach, traveled up past her ribcage, and escaped through her lips. "Of course I will. And I've come to care a great deal for you as well. It took a scheming libertine to set your path on a direct interception with mine, but it took an ever-watchful God to make certain that juncture turned into a parallel journey."

"Guess we both got caught in the tide's strong flow."

"I know one thing though," Grace said with a bright smile. "I look forward to all He has in store for us farther down the line."

"I agree." His eyes darkened, and a telltale gleam entered into them. "And now, with your permission, I'd like to show you just how grateful I am our paths did converge and that our course is set together from this day forward."

Grace licked her lips, her palms again growing sweaty, despite Andrew's firm hold on them. Her breath caught in her throat at his earnest gaze. Unable to voice her agreement, she merely nodded.

Andrew freed one of his hands to cradle her chin. Drawing closer to her, he lowered his lips toward hers. As his mouth touched hers, he conveyed his deepest emotions to her. His kiss captured her lips as well as the rest of her heart.

* * * * *

REQUEST YOUR FREE BOOKS!

2 FREE CHRISTIAN NOVELS
PLUS 2
FREE
MYSTERY GIFTS

HEARTSONG
PRESENTS

REQUEST YOUR FREE BOOKS!

2 FREE INSPIRATIONAL NOVELS
PLUS 2
FREE
MYSTERY GIFTS

Love Inspired

YES! Please send me 2 FREE Love Inspired® novels and my 2 FREE mystery gifts (gifts are worth about $10). After receiving them, if I don't wish to receive any more books, I can return the shipping statement marked "cancel." If I don't cancel, I will receive 6 brand-new novels every month and be billed just $4.49 per book in the U.S. or $4.99 per book in Canada. That's a savings of at least 22% off the cover price. It's quite a bargain! Shipping and handling is just 50¢ per book in the U.S. and 75¢ per book in Canada.* I understand that accepting the 2 free books and gifts places me under no obligation to buy anything. I can always return a shipment and cancel at any time. Even if I never buy another book, the two free books and gifts are mine to keep forever.

105/305 IDN FVW5

Name	(PLEASE PRINT)	

Address		Apt. #

City	State/Prov.	Zip/Postal Code

Signature (if under 18, a parent or guardian must sign)

Mail to the **Reader Service:**
IN U.S.A.: P.O. Box 1867, Buffalo, NY 14240-1867
IN CANADA: P.O. Box 609, Fort Erie, Ontario L2A 5X3

**Are you a subscriber to Love Inspired books
and want to receive the larger-print edition?
Call 1-800-873-8635 or visit www.ReaderService.com.**

* Terms and prices subject to change without notice. Prices do not include applicable taxes. Sales tax applicable in N.Y. Canadian residents will be charged applicable taxes. Offer not valid in Quebec. This offer is limited to one order per household. Not valid for current subscribers to Love Inspired books. All orders subject to credit approval. Credit or debit balances in a customer's account(s) may be offset by any other outstanding balance owed by or to the customer. Please allow 4 to 6 weeks for delivery. Offer available while quantities last.

Your Privacy—The Reader Service is committed to protecting your privacy. Our Privacy Policy is available online at www.ReaderService.com or upon request from the Reader Service.

We make a portion of our mailing list available to reputable third parties that offer products we believe may interest you. If you prefer that we not exchange your name with third parties, or if you wish to clarify or modify your communication preferences, please visit us at www.ReaderService.com/consumerschoice or write to us at Reader Service Preference Service, P.O. Box 9062, Buffalo, NY 14269. Include your complete name and address.

LIDIR12

ReaderService.com

Manage your account online!

- Review your order history
- Manage your payments
- Update your address

We've designed the Reader Service website just for you.

Enjoy all the features!

- Reader excerpts from any series
- Respond to mailings and special monthly offers
- Discover new series available to you
- Browse the Bonus Bucks catalogue
- Share your feedback

Visit us at:

ReaderService.com